Café de Sophia

by

M.A. ALSADAH

Café de Sophia

M.A. Alsadah

ISBN (Print Edition): 978-1-66785-319-2

ISBN (eBook Edition): 978-1-66785-320-8

For my lovely nephews
Adam & Alia

Table of Contents

Acknowledgement

I wouldn't have finished this wonderful journey of writing this book if it wasn't for my wonderful companions that each deserve special thanks and yet I wouldn't have done them justice in doing so.

I would like to thank my best friends Hassan Alajaj and Abdulrahman Hakami who have been true companions in this journey. We would sit together and have long conversations and discussions about some of the topics mentioned in the book. I surely learned from their knowledge and perspective. I'm really blessed to have someone who I can sit and have deep intellectual conversations with.

I would also like to give special thanks to my editor, Katie Zdybel, not only for her superb editorial skills, but also for her thoughtful comments on the conversations and arguments made in the book that helped in reshaping those conversations. She really understood the vision of my book and preserved its soul.

Preface

When I first read some of the work of Plato, I immediately got attached to the Socratic dialogue method of rationalizing, teaching, examining, and sometimes researching a topic intellectually. It is really a fascinating method, the back-and-forth play of logic and reasoning between speakers is at its peak. Plato gave me the love for Philosophy, Wisdom, and Speech, he was the stepping stone for me into the work of other philosophers like Pythagoras, Lao Tzu, and my favorite, Hermes Trismegistus, along with many others of different believes, schools, and religious backgrounds. Plato's work has been my inspiration in writing this book

Writing Cafe de Sophia has been a fascinating journey. A journey through philosophy, knowledge and wisdom that came to an end not because it finished, but because I had to stop it somewhere; for writing such a work is a lifelong journey not easily completed and hardly ever perfected. Cafe de Sophia has been a special work for me. Having something to grow and develop with across a period of time takes a special place in your heart.

In this book, I have quoted from many different books and philosophers and please note that my interpretations of those quotes are not the definitive definitions of what they mean but my personal understanding of them. Here, I'm trying to bring new fresh ideas and perspectives into the topics and trying to divert as much as possible from already established explanations and thoughts. At the end, please consider all of the argumentations and speeches made in the book as my personal research in the discussed topics and that the conclusions achieved are not definitive.

CHAPTER 1

Introduction

People find interest in all sorts of things. And those interests all lay on one spectrum with good on one side and bad on the other side. People say that being on the bad side is the worst thing that could happen to anyone, but that couldn't be further from the truth—at least for me. The way I see it, being in the middle or having no interest at all, is much worse because you don't belong to any side, you are all alone, and you are not passionate about anything. I envy people who are passionate about something and who have found their true calling, whether that thing is good or bad, for they feel a sense of belonging. This may be a sense of belonging to either a group, a hobby, or a critical issue in life.

When I started finding my own way of life, I thought that being in the middle and waiting for something good was a much better position to be in than being on the bad side. But to be honest, I would want anything—good or bad—to move me from where I'm at right now. I am only sixteen years old, but already, I feel like a lost soul with no passion in life.

These are the thoughts in my mind as I walk home from school. I am trapped in a daily routine of lostness and boredom that only goes away when I sleep. On top of this, it has started to rain.

'Great,' I said to myself, hurrying home along the sidewalk. 'I better find a place to stay out of the rain otherwise I'm going to catch a cold.'

I came upon a café, entered in, and took out my phone to make a call.

'Hi Mom, I finished my classes early today,' I said. 'I was walking home, but it started raining heavily all of the sudden. Can you come and pick me up?'

'I'm sorry, honey,' my mother replied, 'I'm afraid I won't be able to leave work and pick you up for an hour.'

'It's OK,' I said. 'I can wait, I'll grab a coffee or something.'

'Good idea,' my mother said. 'What's the address?'

I spotted a barista walking past me. 'Excuse me,' I said, 'what's the name of this café and what's the address please?'

'It's called Café de Sophia,' replied the barista, 'and it is beside the Paris Opera Granier.'

I thanked the barista and gave the address to my mother.

'I won't be late. Have fun!' said my mother.

I had entered the café in a rush, so I hadn't paid much attention to the place. But after ending the call, I took a look around to see myself standing in a crowded, classic café that was long, big, and rectangular in shape with a high ceiling. The sound of the babbling of the crowd and the tinkling of tableware filled the air. I walked forward slowly, looking around, getting lost in the atmosphere, and admiring the place for it had minute, exquisite details.

The left wall of the café had gilded panels that came in a thin, wide, rectangular pattern. The panels were embellished with French Louis XV-style, bronze candlestick sconces whilst colorful frescos adorned the entirety of the wider panels. As for the right wall, a series of tall windows and mirrors filled it. The windows, as tall as they were, didn't extend to the base of the ceiling but rather stopped below, leaving the remaining space to be ornated with a golden garden design that stretched above their window scarfs. There were also white curtains covering the windows. In between the windows that started from the floor, there were large, gilded mirrors that started a bit higher above the floor level and stretched all the way up alongside the windows. The upper frame of the mirrors had an extended ornamentation that was floral in design.

This Rococo interior design that was the emblem of the right-side wall extended all the way up to the ceiling, adorning it with its exquisite architecture. The ceiling was curved and, instead of having frescos painted on it as most common with the Rococo style, it had soft ornamentations that outlined the bases of beautiful crystal chandeliers that spread, equally spaced, at the central line of the café. Also, sculpted moldings of golden colors filled the edges and corners of this multi-layered ceiling. As for the floor, it was made of wood laid down in an interwoven pattern making squares in between the lines, and inside each square, the same pattern was repeated but running in a different angle.

Occupying this great place, were numerous seating areas of various sizes that spread across the café in a random fashion. The seating areas were mainly of two types: the first one came in a different combination of sofas with Bergère or wingback armchairs along with coffee and side tables. The second type had upholstered oval-back chairs or armchairs along with circular, claw-footed tables. All of the furniture was of the Louis XVI design style and had floral toile fabric.

The café was built as a great hall adorned by the exquisite characteristics of the Rococo architecture which is considered highly ornamental, decorative, and theatrical in its design. The brightness of pastel colors was another key element of the Rococo design. This palette, which consisted of a few powdery hues like pearl gray, light yellows, lilacs, and pale blues, helped in bringing the colorful frescos into attention by contrast.

This interior design style of Rococo architecture and Louis XIV furniture brought royalty and class into the café. The café was its own aesthetic universe, where wall and ceiling treatment, art, and decorative elements worked together to create a high-spirited and light atmosphere that made it the perfect backdrop for high-minded aristocrats looking to entertain and impress their guests.

While walking and admiring the café, most of my attention was taken by the frescos on the left-side wall which were of many different themes. Although they were very interesting and required the attention of the viewer, that didn't stop me from skimming past them, and so, without me noticing, I'd reached the other end of the café. On the wall of that end, there was a large fresco that almost stretched across the whole wall. It was obvious that this fresco was the masterpiece and jewel of the café and I just had to stop and examine it.

The painting showed a scenery in what seemed to be in ancient Greek or Rome based on the architecture. At the center, there were two men walking and talking to each other whilst surrounded by numerous people each doing their own thing.

While I was admiring the fresco, I heard someone say, 'It is called "The School of Athens".'

I turned to the direction of the voice to see a man dressed in a suit, sitting alone at a table, and I replied to him with, 'What?'

'The name of the painting you were admiring, "The School of Athens",' said the man.

'It is really stunning,' I said.

'Come over here please, young man,' requested the man.

I approached the man and got a closer look at him. He seemed to be in his early fifties and had short, black hair and a circular-style beard with traces of white strands in it. The man sat comfortably with one foot on top of the other. He had a serious look in his eyes, giving him an air of dignity and prestige.

'Please have a seat,' offered the man with a gentle smile.

'No, thank you,' I said. 'I don't want to disturb you.'

'Please, I insist,' he replied.

I felt that it would be rude to keep refusing and so I pulled out the chair in front of him and sat down.

The man smiled at me. 'What's your name, young man?'

'Nate River,' I replied.

'You have a nice name, mister River, I like it,' the man said. 'As for me, I won't tell you my real name but my friends call me, Plato.'

'Plato?!' I remarked.

Plato smiled gently and said, 'It is a long story, don't worry about it. Anyway, I was hoping to see if one of my friends were here, but I'm failing to see anyone today.'

'"Hoping to see!"' I said. 'You didn't agree to meet them beforehand?' After I said that I noticed that I was questioning a strange man and so I immediately added apologetically, 'I'm sorry! I didn't mean to judge you or question or …'

'Very perceptive, Mr. River!' Plato said, interrupting me.

'What?' I said in a shock after hearing this unexpected reply.

'You see, my friends and I come here occasionally,' said Plato. 'You can say that this is our usual place. Nonetheless, since I don't think that any of them are coming today, you will have to keep me accompanied.'

'I'm glad to sit with you, but what would a man like you want with a boy like me?' I asked.

'Just a simple conversation, nothing more,' Plato answered.

'A conversation?' I asked.

'Don't worry; I promise you'll like it,' said Plato as he raised his hand, calling to a specific person working at the café.

A middle-aged man came to our table. 'Good afternoon, Plato, it's nice to see you, as usual.'

'Likewise, Alfred, likewise,' replied Plato. 'How are you doing today?'

'I'm fine, thank you,' Alfred replied. 'I see you have a new friend today, and a young one at that, is he one of your relatives?'

'Actually, we've just met,' Plato said.

'So, are you going to initiate him?' said Alfred, smiling at me and making me a little confused.

Plato laughed gently and said, 'I hope so.'

'So you do have a new friend!' Alfred said with a smile. 'I'll bring the initiation tea cup!'

'Thank you, Alfred!' Plato said with a gentle smile as Alfred left.

All of this was happening while I stood confused, and a little bit worried, from the odd interaction that took place between two strangers.

'Seeing how perceptive you were earlier,' Plato started speaking to me, 'I take it you noticed that Alfred and I must have known each other for quite a while, right?'

'It is very obvious and nice too,' I said with a smile. 'Also, what did he mean by initiation?'

Plato smiled and said, 'don't mind that, let's get to our conversation, Mr. River.'

'Please call me, Nate,' I requested.

'All right, Nate,' spoke Plato. 'Introduce yourself to me; I'd like to know you.'

Usually, I would be introverted when talking to a stranger but something about Plato made me feel at ease. I felt comfortable and safe with him.

'What do you want to know?' I asked.

Plato took a comfortable sitting position and said, 'Whatever you'd like me to know.'

'Well ... my name is Nate River. I'm 16 years old,' I said. 'I go to school here in Paris and I'm taking game design classes in the afternoon.'

After I finished speaking, I expected Plato to say something, but he didn't and there was a moment of silence in which he was staring at me with eyes full of confidence and seriousness.

After a pause, Plato smiled and said, 'Is that all?'

I replied hesitantly, not knowing what he expected. 'Yes.'

Alfred returned and served us one teapot and two tea cups and Plato thanked him. I noticed the crockery of the café was vintage Royal Albert of floral design.

'Let me ask you this, Nate,' said Plato as he poured some tea for us. 'Would you hit a dog or a cat if it annoys you?'

'What?!' I replied, confused from his question that came out of nowhere.

Plato then asked, 'Or would you commit stealing?'

I replied a little seriously, 'No, of course not! Why would you think that I would do such things?'

'Why wouldn't I? I don't know you, and after all, I'm just saying it as a possibility, not as a certainty,' said Plato.

'I'm a little confused that you would think of me in this way, especially after what I have just told you about myself,' I said.

'You mean your introduction?' asked Plato.

'Yes,' I answered.

Plato took a sip of his tea and said, 'So you think that what you said about yourself shouldn't make me think of you that way?'

'I think it shouldn't,' I replied.

Plato then said, 'I don't blame you for thinking that since you know yourself, but for strangers, they might not necessarily come to your conclusion.'

'I'm not sure I understand what you mean,' I replied.

Plato smiled and asked, 'Tell me, Nate, does going to school in Paris prevent one from committing the acts I mentioned?'

'No, not necessarily,' I answered.

Plato continued, 'And what about the study of game design?'

Seeing where Plato was going with his questions made me take a moment to think and not answer him immediately. 'The same goes to game design,' I said.

'Now, would you blame me for thinking that you would hit an animal or steal a thing?' said Plato.

'I suppose I can't,' I replied.

'To be honest,' spoke Plato, 'you haven't answered my original question in which I wanted to know you.'

'I still don't see where I failed to answer your question,' I said, confused.

'You told me your name and age, which is perfectly fine,' said Plato, 'but then you started telling me about where and what you study, and that's where you went astray from my question.'

'I still don't understand,' I replied.

Plato continued, 'Let's take, for example, a man who went to the top prestigious schools in his early years, and then he graduated with a bachelor's and a master's degree, with honors, from the best universities, and now he is the CEO of a big company. Would you say that this man is a good person or a bad person?'

I replied with, 'Well… since he went to prestigious schools he must be from a prestigious family, which will mean that he would have had the best education, crafts, and skills taught to him. Someone like that I'd say ought to be a good person.'

'Not necessarily,' Plato said, as I reached for my cup of tea for a sip. 'Putting aside the type of education this person has received and how he's implementing it—for these things deserve their own conversation—it is true that having the best educators and tutors may help raise and make a good person, but this is not always the case. Don't you see some of this type of people that receive a prestigious education behave like morons—acting selfish, arrogant, and without pride or honor?'

'It is true that there are people like that, but there are also people with the same circumstances that are humble and with good manners,' I said.

'That is also true,' said Plato.

'So now, is the person good or bad?' I asked, puzzled.

'That's not the point right now,' answered Plato. 'Tell me, if something is always the evidence of another thing and never anything else, what do you call it?'

'A decisive proof?' I answered uncertainly.

Plato continued, 'Correct. And what if something can be the evidence of two or more things—can it be a decisive proof?'

'It cannot be for it carries multiple possibilities,' I said.

'Exactly, and now back to our example,' Plato continued. 'Is going to prestigious schools a decisive proof for being a good person or a bad one? Or can it be a decisive proof in the first place?'

'It cannot be a decisive proof since it can mean more than one thing,' I said.

'Correct, and following this logic,' spoke Plato, 'the same thing can be said about having a bachelor's or a master's degree, and being a CEO of a company; is this not true?'

'It is true,' I replied.

Plato then asked, 'So, will such an introduction help us know this person?'

'Knowing *about him* yes, but *knowing him* no, not in the way we discussed at least,' I answered.

'Well said, Nate!' said Plato happily, making me smile. 'This kind of introduction is not suitable for introducing oneself and can be considered kind of illusive since it can mean many things.'

'Which kind of introduction will you say it is?' I asked.

Plato answered, 'The kind where someone introduces himself by stating his … study or work history, if we can call it that way.'

'I agree with you that knowing the institute that someone studied in does not help in knowing that person,' I said, 'but won't knowing the subjects that he studied be more helpful in knowing him?'

'Let me ask you this,' spoke Plato, 'if someone told you that he studied creative writing, does it decisively mean that he is a creative writer?'

'No,' I replied.

Plato continued, 'And if someone told you that he studied medicine, does it decisively mean that he is professionally a good doctor and not a bad one?'

'No,' I replied.

Plato continued, 'And what if someone told you that he has been practicing painting for the last 15 years, does it mean that he is a good painter or a creative one?'

'But this one is different from the previous two,' I responded. 'Here we have a duration of practice and experience, but at the end, I would need to see some of his work to make a judgement.'

Plato replied, 'At the end, one's years of experience at something are not a decisive proof of something, right?' I agreed and then Plato continued, 'Therefore, the "study or work history", as we called it, does not help in knowing a person since it carries multiple meanings and possibilities, correct?'

'I can agree with you on that, but then why do most people introduce themselves that way if it doesn't tell anything about themselves?' I said.

'Because it does,' replied Plato.

I chuckled and said, 'I'm now confused; didn't we just agree that stating your history of study and work doesn't help others to know you?'

Plato smiled and said, 'You changed the topic without noticing. It will help others to know *about* you, but not to *know* you—for these are two totally different things.'

After a moment of silence, thinking about the difference between the two and not finding it, I replied saying, 'How do I introduce myself then?'

'That's not the right question at the moment,' said Plato.

'What is, then?' I asked.

'Since our main goal is to know a person, then it is only fitting that we look into what makes a person or an individual in the first place,' said Plato. 'So, let me ask you this, what do you think makes a person?'

'I honestly don't know,' I replied.

'Let's get back to the example of the painter,' said Plato. 'Why did you say that you needed to see the painter's paintings first, before making a judgement?'

'Well... I need to see his work before judging his craft,' I replied.

'Good, and can we say that his work is the action resulted from his years of experience?' said Plato.

'Yes,' I replied, getting more interested in the conversation.

Plato continued, 'Then following the same logic, can we say that what makes a person are the actions or doings he is committing?'

'Yes, supposedly,' I replied.

'Thus, if we looked into what kinds of doings are committed by an individual, are they not the physical actions he does and the words he speaks?' asked Plato.

'I think this is right, if you want to bring it to a basic level,' I answered.

'And aren't these two basic things by a more basic name called manners?' said Plato.

Then, thinking that I had the correct answer, I replied eagerly, 'So manners are truly what makes a person, hence the saying "Manners maketh man".'

Plato smiled at my enthusiasm and said, 'I think we are on the right path, but we shouldn't stop here. I see the causes go even deeper.'

'What's deeper than manners?' I asked.

Plato replied, 'Let us investigate what causes manners in the first place, Nate. How are they selected? Based on what? And why would a person choose one manner over another? Answering these questions is surely crucial in helping us with our main point of investigation, which is to know someone.'

'I agree with you, but which question should we start with?' I said.

'Sometimes it is useful to look at things in a simpler manner,' said Plato. 'It is true we have many questions, but they all revolve around the root cause or causes that manners are based on. Let us start from here.' I nodded in agreement and Plato continued, 'Let's take, for example, a football fan, someone who is really loyal to a team. Will he ever cheer another team against his own?'

'No,' I replied.

'Would he miss a match of his team?' said Plato.

'No, never,' I replied.

Plato continued, 'Would he not defend his team during debates even if he knows the point made against his team is correct?'

'For sure he would defend his team,' I said.

Plato then asked, 'Why do you think he would do all of these things?'

'It is because he loves his team,' I answered.

'So, this love dictates the way this fan will behave, in other words, his manners, am I right?' said Plato.

'You are right,' I replied.

'Therefore in this situation, what do you call the thing that guides actions or is the reason behind them?' asked Plato.

'Something like a redline that cannot be crossed, a rule that is always kept, or maybe a principle that is always followed,' I answered.

'Let us go with principle,' said Plato. 'By knowing the principle of love of this fan towards his team, can't we predict what actions he would commit in matters involving his team?'

'Surely, we can,' I replied.

'So, principles are the main thing that drives the actions, whether verbal or physical, of people.' Plato continued, 'A person's manners or actions are based on his principles and knowing those principles will help you predict what that person would do in a particular situation. Is this not what knowing a person is?'

It took a moment for Plato's explanation to sink in and I was glad to hear his deduction, for it was the first logical argument made in the conversation and I found the way of proofing things via this method very beautiful and engaging.

'This all makes sense!' I said excitedly. 'Knowing the principles of someone will make you know him. I think this is the answer to our question.'

'Even though I see us on the right path,' spoke Plato, 'we shouldn't be too quick to claim knowledge of this matter and should look at it from every angle.'

I replied saying, 'What else is there to look into?'

'We said that to know a person is to know the principles he holds, right?' said Plato.

'Yes,' I replied.

Plato continued, 'And we said that knowing those principles will help us know how he would behave in certain situations, right?'

'Yes,' I replied.

Plato continued, 'And when two principles clash with each other, what happens? What will a person do? Do you know?'

'In this case, I'm not sure I know what's going to happen,' I said.

'We seem to have arrived at a point following principles where we still don't know what a person will do, and so we still can't *know* a person,' said Plato.

'Do you think the viewpoint of principles is wrong and we should look into other ways of knowing a person?' I said.

'Not at all, maybe we just need to see what's going to happen when two principles are put against each other and see how the outcome is determined,' said Plato.

'What do you mean?' I asked.

'Imagine a manager having two principles; one for always saying the truth, and another for always achieving higher positions at work.' Plato continued, 'Let's say that this manager is in a situation where if he says the truth he will lose a promotion, and if he lies he will get that promotion. Now, his two principles are put against each other. What do you think the manager would do in this situation; which principle is he going to follow?'

I took a moment to think, in which I observed a barista serving dessert plates with spoons and forks to a nearby table. I noticed that the café cutlery was of classic design as well.

I replied to Plato's question saying, 'I guess he is going to do what he sees is more important to him.'

'Are you speaking about the outcomes here or the principles themselves?' asked Plato.

'The principles of course, since they dictate the actions themselves,' I answered.

'Therefore, he's going to weigh the two principles and the one with more value to him will outweigh the other, correct?' said Plato.

'Yes, that is correct,' I replied.

'We could state then that knowing the principles of a person makes the first half of knowing that person,' spoke Plato, 'and knowing the values of those principles makes the other half; do you agree with this statement?'

'I totally agree with you,' I said, amazed by what we had reached so far.

Plato said, 'Well then, I think we have arrived to a satisfying answer to our question of what makes a person. His principles and values, and by knowing these things you know a person.' I nodded in agreement and Plato continued, 'Let us now get back to the original question I asked you at the beginning of our delightful conversation; would you like to answer it now?'

After a few seconds of thinking, I said, somewhat embarrassed, 'What was the question again?'

Plato smiled gently. 'I asked you to introduce yourself. I wanted to know you and not to know about you.'

'OK, that,' I responded. 'So you want to know my principles and values?'

'Principles don't have to be big things like loyalty, humbleness, or generosity; instead, they can be anything,' said Plato. 'For example, one of the principles of mine is that I would never smoke a cigarette, but I could never say no to a cigar.'

I laughed at his statement and said, 'Why is that?'

Plato answered with a smile, 'I find them too tiny for my hand and they leave a disgusting smell in the mouth and breath.'

I then said, 'What other principles do you have? Introduce yourself to me for I'd like to know you; you seem interesting.'

'I will go first, but don't think for a second that you're off the hook; you're still answering my question.' I smiled and Plato continued, 'I love speech and talking with other people either in discourses, debates, or in simple conversations. I would never say no to a conversation and I love to hear new perspectives and opinions, especially those who go against mine. I see the mind as the most valuable thing a human has and only through speech, along with writing, is it ever translated and known.'

Plato's introduction delighted me and made me like him even more. It was the first time that I'd met someone who considered talking—a thing that I've never paid attention to— so passionately. Having the chance to speak and having someone who showed interest in what I had to say, regardless if it was right or wrong, gave me a comfortable, nice feeling.

'So, Nate,' said Plato interrupting my thoughts, 'how about you? Tell me a principle of yours.'

I was about to answer Plato, but nothing came to my mind. I took a few seconds to think, but still nothing, and that's when it hit me: I didn't really know myself. I didn't know what my principles and values were or if I even had some to begin with.

'Honestly, Plato,' I said, shocked by my revelation, 'I don't know. I don't know what my principles are. Is that fine or is there something wrong with me?'

Plato laughed from the bottom of his heart and said, whilst removing traces of tears with a napkin, 'I haven't laughed like this for a long time; thank you, Nate!'

I didn't respond, but I was happy to see him laugh like this.

'It is totally fine,' spoke Plato. 'Don't expect to know yourself at this age. You are still young and there are lots of experiences you have yet to face that will shape you as a person and define your principles and values.'

'But I couldn't come up with a single principle and that saddens me,' I said.

'It is totally fine,' said Plato. 'At this age, I don't totally know myself yet. Knowing one's self is a life journey. You only have to choose carefully and mindfully the principles you want to obtain and the ones you want to neglect. Principles can be both good and bad, so choose wisely.'

Then, all of a sudden, my phone rang and after looking at the caller ID I said sadly, 'It's my mother. She is outside the café right now, ready to pick me up.'

'Well, Nate, talking to you has been a real pleasure,' said Plato. 'Thank you for the wonderful conversation.'

At that moment, I felt that I needed the company of someone like Plato in my life. I never thought that a well-spoken conversation would impact me this way. Before, I was searching for a purpose in life and, after having conversed with Plato, I felt like he could help me with that quest. I didn't know how and why, but what I was sure of was that I wasn't ready to let go of such a man yet. I wanted to have more conversations with him, to know what it was that affected me this much.

'It was really pleasant talking to you too, Plato,' I said, 'but I feel that I really want to meet you once more. I don't want to leave today and never see you again.'

Plato smiled and said, 'I'm really glad that you liked our conversation and even more glad that you want to have more. Tell you what, why don't you come next Friday night at 8pm here. My friends and I are having a conversation that I think you would like.'

I responded with happiness saying, 'Thank you very much; I'd really love to meet your friends and hear more of your conversations.'

We exchanged phone numbers and exited the café together. As I entered my mother's car, I felt lucky to meet such a person and couldn't wait for the next time I'd meet Plato and his friends. I was so eager for the conversation that would take place. At last, I felt a changing moment had happened in my life, and a beautiful one at that.

CHAPTER 2

Knowledge

A lot of times when you are the eldest son in the family, you get a lot of errands dropped on you when you least want them, and that's exactly what happened to me the night I was to meet with Plato.

When I arrived to the café, I saw Plato on the outside terrace of the café, sitting at a table with three other people. And as I slowly approached the table, I thought to myself, *Oh great, I wanted to come early so I could meet Plato's friends one by one. Now I have to meet them all at the same time. I hate moments like this.*

'You're finally here, welcome, Nate!' said Plato standing up.

'Hello again, Plato,' I greeted back.

Plato started introducing his friends to me, beginning with the one sitting to his right side. 'This young charming lady is Hypatia. Next to her is Protagoras and then Luqman. Everyone, this is Nate, the boy I spoke to you about.'

I exchanged greetings with Plato's friends.

'These are not our real names,' spoke Hypatia. 'They are only the nicknames we go by.'

'Plato never told me the reason behind the nicknames,' I said.

'That's a subject for another time,' said Plato. 'Please, have a seat.'

I sat beside Plato.

'Listen, Nate,' Plato said, whispering to me, 'why were you late? I thought you wouldn't come?'

'Sorry about that,' I whispered back. 'My mother asked me to do some stuff at the last minute.'

'And did you do those things?' asked Plato.

'Yes, I did,' I answered.

Plato said, 'Good, because if you hadn't, I would've sent you back to do them.' I chuckled and Plato continued. 'Anyway, during the conversation tonight, I'd like to ask you to please be quiet and listen, but don't participate. Not quite yet. I'll be happy to answer any questions you might have at a later time; are you OK with that?'

'No problem,' I responded in an even l tone; truthfully, I was so happy for his request, thank god he'd said it and not me. I was glad to speak with Plato again, but with all of these new, grown-up people, it would be hard for me to open up and speak freely.

Before the start of the conversation, I took a moment to observe the café's exterior. As the interior design was of classical style, the exterior was no exception. The long windows ran all over the wall. They were the main attraction of the café architecture. They had round arches with floral sculptures above and, in between the windows, there was a pair of pillars that reached to the base of the roof. I considered myself lucky to have seen the café's exterior at night, for the long windows let the golden rays of the interior lighting come outside in a beautiful fashion that stole the show. The white of the building helped in enhancing that expression.

'Lady and gentlemen,' Plato started speaking to the rest of the group at the table, 'allow me to choose the topic of discussion for this night. It is one that has been spoken about before countless times and many have tried to put a definition to it, even the philosopher Plato had his share of it. A lot of attempts have been made, but none of them meet my satisfaction. Some were unconvincing and others helped rule out possibilities but never gave a fully satisfying answer. I'm speaking about Knowledge. What is Knowledge? I would love for us to combine our minds tonight and try to find a satisfying definition to this great question. I tried to think of it on my own, but fearing being led astray with my own beliefs, I saw that it fits better if many great, unbiased, thinking minds shared their thoughts and perspectives on the matter.'

Seeing how my last conversation with Plato amazed me, I was very interested to see how would a thought-provoking topic as Knowledge unravel.

'Excellent choice, Plato,' spoke Protagoras. 'I've always wanted to think about Knowledge but never had the chance, the free time, or the suitable company to discuss it with. And for these reasons, please allow me to begin the discussion with a statement of my own to what I think Knowledge is.'

'Please do,' said Plato.

Protagoras, a man with short brown hair and an anchor-style beard, who seemed in his mid-thirties, said, 'Knowledge can be personal and collective, right and wrong, true and false, single and multiple, subjective and objective, many things that either agree or disagree with each other, and because of the wide range that Knowledge has and its capability to be many things at once, agreeable or disagreeable, I see it very closely related to perception. And now after I've stated my statement, please allow me to elaborate and explain why I said it.

'We all perceive things differently, and the way we perceive is affected by our beliefs and viewpoints which lead us into having different and sometimes opposing knowledge. Take, for example, a dessert that was tasted by two people; one found it sweet, the other sour. And later when they were asked how it tasted, they both will tell of their own experience, which will be their knowledge of it. You can't say that one is right and the other is wrong, or one has knowledge of the dessert and the other doesn't. Or someone who never tasted the dessert gave an answer out of what he has heard his friend say or the majority say about its taste. You can't state that such person who took others' experience and Knowledge into his own as having no Knowledge or someone with a Knowledge that goes against that of the majority as the same for he is speaking about his own viewpoint and perception.

'There is no one correct answer when it comes to knowing things. And since it is affected by beliefs, viewpoints, and personal experiences, it is only fitting to say that Knowledge is perception.'

Protagoras ended his speech. I found it wonderful and very logical. I thought he had found the answer and the discussion had ended.

'Well said, Protagoras,' spoke Hypatia, the youngest looking person in the group. 'I see why you would relate knowledge with perception, but I'm going to have to disagree with you on that one. It is true that perception can differ in how we know things, but perception is only an instrument for gaining knowledge. Perceiving things is the first step of knowing them. It is only a means of obtaining Knowledge, not Knowledge itself.

'Knowledge can only be one thing never more, an objective fact not a changing belief, an immortal truth not a collective falseness. And for these reasons, Knowledge can only be one already established truth that humanity has strived, and still does, for obtaining it no matter the cost.

'Knowledge is science and science can never be many or opposing, it is one and agreeing. If Knowledge is as you say it is, Protagoras, then trial and error would be meaningless. If anyone did any experiment and his result was taken as a true part of Knowledge, then we wouldn't have arrived to the state of technological and scientific development we are now at.

'If the many are parts of Knowledge, the same and opposing are parts of Knowledge, the true and false are parts of Knowledge as well, then there is no room for ignorance and it is only through admitting and recognizing ignorance that we can even know Knowledge. There is only one way a biological system operates, one way chemicals react with each other, and one solution to math equations.'

With this, Hypatia ended her speech. No matter how convincing Protagoras' logic seemed to me at first, now after hearing Hypatia's, I saw it as more logical and convincing. I found it interesting how my opinion about the matter was changed with each speech made and I wanted to hear what Plato and Luqman had to say.

'I agree with what you just said, Hypatia,' spoke Protagoras. 'But what you have just defined is Scientific Knowledge and not Knowledge as a whole.'

'How would you relate the two of them, Knowledge and Scientific Knowledge?' asked Hypatia.

'I would say,' replied Protagoras, 'that Scientific Knowledge is a part of Knowledge, like a branch from a tree.'

'So what's the difference between the parts and the whole?' said Hypatia.

'The whole helps in containing and stabilizing many parts while the parts help in detailing and emphasizing the whole,' said Protagoras.

'And while emphasizing,' said Hypatia, 'will the parts go against or oppose the core features of the whole?'

'No, this can't be,' replied Protagoras. 'The parts will give more details with accordance to the core principles of the whole—never against them for they are parts of the core principles, and one can't go against his own principle, taking free will out of the equation.'

'I recall that you agreed with the definition I gave to Knowledge earlier, am I right?' said Hypatia.

Protagoras replied, 'Yes, but as to Scientific Knowledge and not Knowledge as a whole.'

'You said that Knowledge can be many, opposing, and subjective,' Hypatia continued, 'and I said that Knowledge can only be one, agreeing, and objective. Why do you agree with both statements, along with identifying your definition as a whole and mine as a part, whilst also saying that the part could never oppose the core principles of the whole it was created from? Can you not see the contradiction you're in?'

Protagoras closed his eyes and went into a deep dive in his mind whilst everybody else either looked at him to hear his response or were deep in their own thoughts themselves. As for me, I was so happy just seeing this back and forth in logic and reasoning. I never thought that a game of words could be this exciting.

Finally, Protagoras opened his eyes and said, 'You are absolutely right, Hypatia, with your definition of Scientific Knowledge, but where you see me in a contradiction, I see myself in a paradox instead.'

'What do you mean?' asked Plato.

'While I agree with Hypatia's statement,' continued Protagoras, 'I cannot see the falseness in mine. Perception is an individual's knowledge and not only a means to Knowledge. You cannot dismiss someone's perception as Knowledge just because he came to incorrect information. After all, it is his own perception of it and he sees it as real Knowledge.'

'Knowledge is Science,' said Hypatia, 'and in science there is only one truth.'

'What about if a scientist got some part of science wrong?' spoke Plato. 'Would you consider that part of scientific Knowledge or not?'

'If it's wrong, of course not,' answered Hypatia.

Plato then said, 'but what about the period of time where that science was believed to be true, will it be Knowledge or not?'

Hypatia cracked a smile as if she knew where Plato was going with his question and said, 'It would be called Knowledge.'

Plato continued, 'And after the discovery of its falseness?'

'It would be called false knowledge,' said Hypatia.

'And a scientific one at that?' Hypatia nodded in agreement and Plato continued saying, 'Now, your own definition accommodated right and wrong.'

'I guess we need to keep digging into the matter even further,' said Hypatia. 'How naïve of me to think that the answer could be simple.'

'No worries,' spoke Plato, 'we only need to investigate the matter in new viewpoints.'

'Or maybe a new cultural perspective is just what we need,' said Luqman.

'What do you mean, Luqman?' asked Plato.

I turned to the man sitting to my left. He seemed at the prime of his youth. He had short black hair and a stubble-style beard. Luqman replied to Plato saying, 'In the Arabic Language, there are two words that are translated to English as Knowledge; "Ma'rifa" and "Elm". The first word is associated with Knowledge whilst the second word is more associated with… as you named it "Scientific Knowledge". The two words are totally different, they don't relate to each other in terms of parts and wholes, and they have different uses.

'Let me elaborate more. The Arabic Language is a language of roots. Each root has its own unique meaning and can be shaped into nouns, adjectives, verbs, and so on, of different grammatical numbers. Let us now create two roots in the English language and conjugate them. The first is *Knowledge* and the second is *Science*. If I wanted to teach you something within the domain of Knowledge, I would be knowledge-ing you, making the root a verb. And if I wanted to teach you something within the domain of Science, I would be science-ing you.

'You see, where the domains of Knowledge and Science might be intertwined and the same to an English speaker, especially with the word "teach" being used for both of them, they are completely different from each other to an Arabic speaker.

'I think it would be very helpful if we looked at Knowledge and Scientific Knowledge as two separate things, like in the Arabic Language, instead of seeing them as two opposing meanings fighting for domination.'

'I'm very glad to be your friend, Luqman!' Plato said with a smile. 'I think taking your approach is the best option we have right now, especially when I see that both Protagoras' and Hypatia's statements hold some form of truth into them and, as Protagoras named it, I need to get out of this paradox I'm in right now.'

This was my thought as well. I had never thought that looking into things from a different cultural perspective could make a big difference and now, I was more drawn to the conversation than ever.

'So, Plato,' spoke Hypatia, 'are you saying that Protagoras' statement is related to Knowledge and mine is related to Science?'

'This could be the case but,' spoke Luqman, 'we can't jump into conclusions so quickly without first answering some key questions here about Knowledge and Science to figure out what are they and how they differentiate from one another. Questions like, how are they obtained? What are their boundaries and domains? Where and when does one end and the other start?'

'Excellent choice of questions, Luqman!' said Plato.

Luqman thanked Plato and said, 'How is Knowledge obtained? How do we begin to know things in the first place?'

'We know things by the way we perceive them,' said Protagoras. 'It could be firsthand by seeing or examination, or secondhand by hearing or reading someone else's experience.'

'Let's take a person, for example,' said Luqman. 'How would you perceive him?'

'By seeing him,' said Protagoras, 'touching him, or hearing about him.'

'How did you perceive in the first place,' said Luqman, 'what are the tools you used in your perception?'

'In this case, I would say my five senses,' replied Protagoras.

'If it is through the senses that we are able to perceive things,' said Luqman, 'then our perception will shape and determine the type of Knowledge we have of them, right?'

'That seems to be the case,' replied Protagoras.

'We agree that the senses perceive Knowledge,' said Luqman. 'We now need to know which type of Knowledge it perceives so we get some idea of what Knowledge is, if this is the logic we ought to go with?'

'It is, necessarily,' replied Protagoras.

'I see the account that you gave earlier is most suitable here, Protagoras,' said Luqman. 'Senses are not of equal perception among people. They differentiate from one person and another, from the healthy and the sick, from the young and the old. Their strength might vary between people and can be filtered through their beliefs, assumptions, and deduction capabilities.

'With senses being the way of knowledge and having the features we spoke of earlier, then we can say that Knowledge, as you said earlier, can be both subjective and objective, true and false, singular, and multiple. It all depends on how the sensor perceives it, whether his perception is right or wrong. How do you find our deduction so far?'

'It is very logical,' replied Protagoras.

Luqman continued, 'With this said, we can conclude that knowledge is obtained through the senses and its boundaries start and end with the perceptional limitation of the five senses. Now we must turn our attention to Science and apply to it the same thought process we did with Knowledge.'

'Let's start by taking how the word science is defined,' spoke Hypatia. 'Science is the systematic knowledge of the physical or material world gained through observation and experimentation.'

'So then,' spoke Luqman, 'how is science obtained? What are the tools used to obtain it?'

'To put it simply,' started Hypatia, 'science is obtained through seeing, testing, and demonstrating which are performed through the senses. This mighty be a tricky part to solve.'

'Not necessarily,' said Luqman. 'We've agreed that Knowledge is only gained through the senses, and what could the senses perceive? Only the appearances of things, never anything in a deeper level and that's where we mark its boundaries. And so, if we want to define Science, we need to see what lies beyond the senses. What is the next step that comes after sensing something or knowing it?'

'In this case,' started Hypatia, 'I will go back to a point I made earlier, that perception is just a means to Scientific Knowledge, or Science as we're calling it now. Science is objective, meaning that it has only one unchanging truth. And since Science is obtained through means via the senses, the question is what are the available tools for us humans to use that can do what the senses can't?'

'Let us review the actions done by humans,' Luqman started. 'If seeing, hearing, smelling, tasting, and touching or physical actions are all done by the five senses, there are still extra actions that might be helpful in answering our questions. Such actions are thinking, which is done by the mind, and feeling, which is done by the heart.'

'I think our answer lies in the mind,' said Hypatia. 'As we said earlier, the five senses can only give us the appearances of things, they can never reach the information that lies beyond the realm of the senses, like how things operate. Such things can only be reached or deduced by the thinking mind.

'Take the digestive system as an example: it consists simply of the mouth, the esophagus, the stomach, the two intestines, and the anus at the end. Dissecting the human body and examining these parts through the senses will only lead you to know the physical attributes of them: their shape, location, consistency, and so on. The senses will never lead you to know how these parts operate on their own and as a whole. Such a task can only be known by doing some experimentation, the results of which are known by the senses, and then arriving to their functionality through the thinking mind.'

'I agree with your supposition,' said Luqman. 'Knowledge is about knowing the points through the senses, while connecting those points is done by Science through the thinking mind.'

'Exactly,' replied Hypatia.

Luqman continued, 'If the tool of Science is the mind, what will be its domain or boundaries? When does it start and end?'

'If we have laid the boundaries of Knowledge based on its tool,' started Hypatia, 'then we ought to think the same of Science. In this case, what is the limit of the mind? I don't know if such a limit exists, so we may say that the boundaries of Science are all that the mind can comprehend.'

'Maybe we need to look at this from a different angle,' spoke Luqman. 'Instead of looking at the limit of the tool, let us look at the limit of the topic itself, which is Science.'

'What do you mean?' asked Hypatia.

'What is the main purpose of Science?' said Luqman. 'Why do we seek it in the first place?'

'To know the operations of things,' said Hypatia.

'So, can we state that the domain and boundaries of Science lies within how things work and operate?' asked Luqman.

'I think that's a correct and a direct statement,' replied Hypatia.

'With the tool and boundaries of Science known,' said Luqman, 'can we finally define what Science is?'

'Science is the systematic knowledge of the physical world that shows the operations of its general laws,' said Hypatia.

'We are in agreement that the tool used to acquire Science is the mind, are we not?' said Luqman.

'Yes,' replied Hypatia.

'So then, is the mind limited only to the material world?' said Luqman. 'Can it not be used to deduce and know the operations of the incorporeal things like dreams, souls, and the unseen parts of the universe and so on?'

'Some of the means in which the mind operates are reasoning, deduction, and rational thinking.' Hypatia continued, 'I don't see any reason for such means to be tied to the physical and material world.'

'Well said!' praised Luqman.

'Therefore, Science will be the systematic or operational knowledge of the universe,' said Hypatia.

'Protagoras,' said Luqman, 'can you put what we learned about Knowledge so far in a direct and correct statement?'

'Of course,' spoke Protagoras. 'The domain and boundaries of Knowledge lie within what things are.'

'Now, after we have defined both of Knowledge and Science to a satisfying degree,' said Luqman, 'why don't we see what the difference is between the two of them.'

'Since Knowledge is gained through the five senses,' started Protagoras, 'that makes it associated with the appearances of things, which tell us what things are and how we perceive them. Thus making Knowledge perceptible to be many things, at the same time, even if they were opposing to each other. Science, on the other hand, is gained through the mind by diving deep past appearances to the operational level of things. It deals with the single universal truth of how a thing operates.

'When we begin to learn and study about things, we are first introduced to them via our senses; we learn about what they look like and what they are. Only after gaining Knowledge can we apply deduction to reach their operations and how they work—basically, their Science.

'For this, Knowledge is different from Science and their boundaries don't cross. Science comes after Knowledge but not necessarily above it. They are on an equal level.'

'Let us summarize what we came to in simple statements,' said Luqman. '"What is it?" is Knowledge. "How is it?" is Science.'

Luqman's summarizations astonished me, everything was so simple and clear that I wondered how I'd failed to see it in the first place.

'Nicely put, Luqman,' spoke Plato. 'I like how you emphasized what type of question Knowledge and Science answer; it opens up more possibilities. We shouldn't stop our conversation here.'

'What do you mean, Plato?' asked Luqman.

'Can Knowledge answer questions regarding, *how*?' asked Plato.

'As we have defined it, no' replied Luqman.

'How about Science, can it answer questions regarding, *what*?' said Plato.

'Also, no,' replied Luqman.

Plato then said, 'So Knowledge and Science have their own particular field of knowledge or information associated with them, and they don't stray from this, correct?'

'Yes, that is correct,' replied Luqman.

'Let's see then,' Plato continued, 'if *what* is associated with Knowledge, and *how* is associated with Science, what is associated with *why*?'

Luqman took a moment of thinking and said, 'I'm not sure what but I don't see Knowledge or Science fitting into it.'

'Let's not jump into conclusions so quickly,' said Plato. 'We need first to see what kind of question is *why* asking? What kind of answer is needed? And which field is associated with it?'

'This is most necessary, Plato,' said Luqman.

'Let us start then,' spoke Plato. 'When you ask why, what are you asking for exactly and what kind of answer are you expecting?'

'Well, we use *why* when we want to know the motives and causes of things or actions,' said Luqman.

'Very good,' said Plato, 'and when you're asking for the motives or causes, aren't you asking for the reasons behind them, basically?'

'Yes,' replied Luqman.

'So, we agree that *why* is asking about the reasons of things, right?' asked Plato.

'Yes,' replied Luqman.

'So then, what type of reasons are we looking for?' asked Plato.

'Well, when I ask why I want to know why things are the way they are and why actions have happened or are happening in the first place,' answered Luqman.

'Are you speaking about existential reasoning or causative reasoning?' asked Plato.

'Both,' replied Luqman.

'Let us see then, if reason and causation belong to the particular fields of either Knowledge or Science,' said Plato.

'Go ahead,' replied Luqman.

'Let us start with Knowledge first,' spoke Plato. 'Knowledge is associated with what things are, their physical attributes, and known superficial information about them. It is never associated with why they exist in the first place. Secondly, while it is true that Science goes deeper into incorporeal and obscure things, it doesn't answer the question of their existence or causation, only how they operate.

'At the end, when examining if both Knowledge and Science can lead to reason and causation, we found that neither of them does. This can only mean that there is an important field, other than Knowledge or Science, that we ought to figure out.'

'That is necessary,' said Luqman.

'Do you have any suggestions for our mysterious friend?' Asked Plato.

'Could this be the field of Philosophy,' answered Luqman, 'knowing the existential reason of things?'

'Interesting choice, let us examine it,' said Plato. 'What is Philosophy associated with?'

'Giving the name of Philosophy itself, I'd say it is associated with Wisdom,' said Luqman.

'That is correct, and does knowing the reason or causation of things makes someone wise?' asked Plato.

'I think it is a part of it but not all of it,' answered Luqman.

'Why do you say that?' said Plato.

'Wisdom is more complicated than just answering a question of *why*. It is more than just intellect,' said Luqman.

'You're implying that there is something missing—what is it?' said Plato.

'Action,' spoke Luqman. 'Wisdom is about having intellect and, more importantly, what you do with that intellect. How you choose to use and act with it.'

'So you're saying that Wisdom is on an even higher level than what we're looking for?' asked Plato.

'Yes,' replied Luqman.

'In that case,' spoke Plato, 'we need to think of the matter from another angle.'

'Necessarily,' said Luqman.

Plato then said, 'Let's apply the same thought process we did when finding Knowledge and Science. Let's try to see what is the tool used for knowing why things exist.'

Luqman replied, 'I would say that the tool of this unknown field is the thinking mind.'

'I would agree with that,' said Plato.

'But now it seems that we have one tool used for two things, Science and this unknown field,' said Luqman.

'Is there a rule that prevents the mind being used for more than one thing?' asked Plato.

'No, there isn't,' answered Luqman.

'OK, since both Science and this unknown field use the mind,' started Plato, 'let us examine how each of them use it. When you want to know how something works or operates, what kind of process do you use?'

'Experimentation,' said Luqman. 'I'll do a couple of experiments or tests, see the outcomes, and then use my mind to analyze the results to deduce a logical explanation.'

'Very good,' said Plato. 'And when it comes to knowing the reason of things or why they exist, what kind of process will you do?'

'Well,' Luqman started speaking, 'when it comes to the cause and reason of things, there are no experiments and tests involved, only thoughts and perspectives. And so, the process here will be implementing intellect and deep thinking into finding an answer for the question of *why*.'

'And what's the act of deep thinking called?' Asked Plato.

'I'm not sure I know what you mean,' replied Luqman.

'When you spend hours, nights, and days thinking deeply about something,' said Plato, 'and when you take time for yourself and isolate just to find an answer, isn't that the act of contemplation?'

'Yes, it is,' said Luqman. 'I think we might have found the name of this unknown field.'

'We can't be too quick to judge,' said Plato, 'there is one problem here.'

'What is that problem?' Asked Luqman.

'Contemplation is a general term,' said Plato. 'Even Science requires contemplation to be obtained. We need a more specific term for the action of thinking about the existence or cause of things.'

'That is true,' said Luqman.

'What do we look for when contemplating about the existence and cause of things?' asked Plato.

'For the reason behind them,' answered Luqman.

'Therefore, the specific term is Reasoning?' said Plato.

'It could be,' replied Luqman, 'but we should examine it first.'

'We should,' said Plato. 'Does Reasoning answers the question of *why*?'

'Yes, it does,' replied Luqman.

Plato continued, 'And does it interfere with the domains of Knowledge and Science? Is it associated with the questions of *what* and *how*?'

'It doesn't seem to do so,' said Luqman. 'Reasoning has its specific field of knowledge, knowing the reason behind things or actions.'

'I think it is safe to say that the term is Reasoning,' said Plato.

'I think so too,' said Luqman.

'In summary,' spoke Plato, '"What is it?" is Knowledge, "How is it?" is Science, "Why is it?" is Reasoning. What do you think of our definitions so far?'

'I think our examinations were comprehensive and our conclusions are logical,' said Luqman.

'You really did a great job investigating Reasoning,' praised Protagoras.

'I agree,' said Hypatia, 'but we shouldn't stop our examination yet.'

'What else is there to investigate?' asked Plato.

'Wisdom,' answered Hypatia. 'We need to find out what Wisdom is. What is its tool? And what is its domain?'

'You are right!' said Plato. 'Do you have an idea of where we should start our investigation?'

Hypatia replied, 'I think taking what Luqman said about Wisdom is a good point to start with; he suggested that Wisdom has intellect and action as parts of it.'

'But before we start from that assumption,' said Plato, 'shouldn't we verify that it is correct in the first place lest we be led astray by our assumption?'

'That we should,' replied Hypatia.

'Now,' spoke Plato, 'let us connect the dots we've drawn of Knowledge, Science, and Reasoning to see if we can map a road to Wisdom. We first become introduced to things by our five senses and only then through Knowledge of them may we deduce their operations. And, in turn, only through knowing Science of things can we deduce the reason of their existence or occurrence.

'Meaning that, you cannot know the Science of things without having Knowledge of them and you cannot know their Reasoning without knowing their Science. Every field we've studied so far needs the others to exist and they all build on top of each other.

'Just like a ladder, every step introduces one new field of knowledge and that field introduces one aspect of knowledge as well. Knowledge, the first step, introduces knowing things in general, Science introduces functionality, and Reasoning introduces the reason or the necessity of things.

'Following this pattern, and if we are to put Wisdom at the top of the ladder, what will Wisdom introduce?'

'As we said earlier,' said Hypatia, 'it would be actions.'

'But actions are a part of every other step of knowledge we mentioned,' said Plato. 'So, what type of action do you mean?'

'I'm not really sure I get what you mean,' said Hypatia.

'We said earlier that Wisdom consists of intellect and action,' said Plato, 'and the type of action associated with Wisdom is that which is based on, or is influenced by, intellect.'

'But that brings another question: what type of intellect is Wisdom associated with?' said Hypatia.

'In our ladder representation,' spoke Plato, 'we put Knowledge or knowing as the first step, next step is Science, followed by the step of Reasoning, and then, at last, we placed Wisdom. And we said that one needs Knowledge to obtain Science. And he needs Science to obtain Reasoning. Meaning, to get to the higher or next step of the ladder of knowledge, one needs to climb the previous step.

'By this logic, since Wisdom is placed at the top of the ladder, obtaining or learning all of the previous types of knowledge is necessary to gain Wisdom. Thus, now we need to see what kind of knowledge does Knowledge, Science, and Reasoning give?

'If you obtain Knowledge, you'll know what something is. If you obtain the Science of something, you'll know how to use it. If you obtain the Reasoning of something, you'll know why it exists in the first place. And if you have all these three types of knowledge about something, you will know the right and wrong ways of doing something.'

'How did you arrive to that conclusion?' asked Hypatia.

'If you know the reason behind something, you'll know the correct time or when to use it. Taking ACs for example, they are made to keep one cool during hot weather, but if you don't know this and you use one during cold weather, you will end up sick with a cold. Thus, by not knowing the Reasoning behind the invention, you use it incorrectly.'

'I get it now,' said Hypatia, 'but how does this help us understand what Wisdom is?'

Plato replied, 'Between knowing right from wrong, and doing right or wrong, are four possibilities. Let's explore them together, all of us, in a general example.'

'Go ahead,' said Protagoras.

Plato said, 'When someone doesn't know right from wrong and he does the wrong thing, what do you call such a person?'

'Ignorant,' said Luqman.

'Correct,' Plato continued, 'and when someone doesn't know right from wrong and he does the right thing, what do you call such a person?'

'A fool,' said Protagoras.

'Correct,' Plato continued, 'and when someone knows right from wrong and he does the wrong thing, what do you call such a person?'

'An egoist—someone who follows his ego, lust, and desires,' said Luqman.

'Correct,' Plato continued, 'and when someone knows right from wrong and he does the right thing, what do you call such a person?'

'A wise man,' said Hypatia.

'Correct,' said Plato, 'now, to put it all together, when someone doesn't know right from wrong and he does the wrong thing, he is truly ignorant for lacking such knowledge. But if he does the right thing while ignorant of what's right and wrong, he is truly a fool for not knowing the value of the thing he just did, which is the right thing, and he shouldn't be called a lucky person, for luck has no place in Knowledge and its implementation.

'And when someone who knows right from wrong and chooses willingly to do the wrong thing, he can be called many names, but most suitably, as Luqman said, an egoist for choosing to neglect righteousness and to follow his own desires. Advice and guidance won't work with such a person, for the reason for doing wrong is not because of ignorance of what is right but because there is no incentive for him to do it. This is really a fatal disease to the soul and only the person himself can cure it.

'As for the person who knows right from wrong and does the right thing at the right time, he is truly wise. There is no standard for what is right and wrong. Knowing the right thing to do at a given situation is a feature for those who are wise, for an action can be right for one situation and wrong for another. Thus, we see here that Wisdom is more about manners and conduct than informatic knowledge alone. Wisdom, then, is the intellect, resulted from all of the previous types of Knowledge, along with doing what's right at the right time.

'Take the act of laughter, which indicates happiness most likely, for example. Laughing in a wedding is considered a good thing but the same can't be said when is done in a funeral. Also, the opposite can be said about crying, which indicates sadness. Crying in a funeral is considered good whilst done in a wedding can be considered as wrong.'

'Well said, Plato!' complemented Luqman.

'Thank you,' said Plato. 'Have we finished looking at all aspects of knowledge or is there something left to discuss?'

'I think there is nothing left,' said Hypatia.

'I believe so too,' said Protagoras.

'Then,' said Plato, 'why don't we summarize briefly what we have arrived at, concerning all types of Knowledge?'

'Can I do it?' I asked shyly, with a quiet voice.

Everyone looked at me with a smile, which made me feel even more shy, and Plato responded to me saying, 'Please do, we're all ears.'

I started speaking with my hands shaking under the table. 'Knowledge is knowing what something is. Science, or scientific knowledge, is knowing how something works or operates. Reasoning is knowing why things are the way they are or why they exist. Lastly, Wisdom is knowing right from wrong and doing what's right.' After I finished my summary, no one said anything and I felt they were expecting me to say more and so I added, 'That's it.'

Upon hearing my last words, everyone smiled and Hypatia said, 'Very good, Nate. I'm glad you liked our conversation and found it interesting, otherwise you wouldn't have made a correct summary.'

Hypatia's words made me shy and I didn't know what to say.

'I think we have arrived to the end of our discussion tonight,' said Plato.

'This was looong... but fun,' said Luqman.

'Sure, it was. Anyway, I'm feeling hungry, who's up for dessert?' asked Hypatia.

'We all are!' said Protagoras.

'Great! Let's call somebody over here,' said Hypatia.

Plato then started talking to me in a low tone saying, 'Did you like tonight's conversation?'

'Do you have to ask?' I said, 'It was very interesting.' I really liked it. I never thought that talking could be that interesting and entertaining.

'I'm glad you liked it,' said Plato.

'One question though,' I said, 'does the group gather every weekend?'

'Not really,' said Plato. 'Our group is much bigger than the people you saw tonight. We all have busy lives and during our free time we come to this café hoping that we may run into each other. It's not like we schedule a meeting.'

I responded, 'But when I first met you, you said that you are meeting your friends tonight. I thought you had an agreement with them.'

'We kind of did,' Plato said. 'We said to our whole group that there will be a gathering tonight and whoever is free should come and join. I came not knowing who exactly was going to show up.'

'I understand now,' I said.

'So you can do the same,' said Plato.

'But what if I don't see you?' I asked.

'Don't worry,' said Plato. 'The group knows you now. If you see anyone you can join him or her. And also, if we're having a gathering just like tonight, I will contact you beforehand.'

'Thank you, really!' I said.

A man came to take our orders and the group started telling him what they wanted. As all of this was happening, I started reflecting on tonight's topic and how Wisdom could truly elevate a person as it touched on both knowledge and manners, which are the components that valuate a mind. Plato's words on the mind as the most valuable thing in a person never appeared truer to me than now and I started seeing Wisdom as a worthy cause to strive after. I also found that Plato and his friends were my way and guide into gaining Wisdom and so, I was so happy and excited to think of the future discussions and what topics I might learn about.

CHAPTER 3

Justice & Equality

The next week, I was sitting by myself in the crowded café. It was a weekend, clouds covered the sun and a gentle breeze filled the air. It was a nice day that no one would miss by sitting at home, myself included.

As I sat alone, I began to contemplate on what the group had discussed last time: Wisdom and how to obtain it. It is true they mentioned that Knowledge, Science, and Reasoning all contribute to gaining Wisdom, but still, I felt that wasn't clear enough an answer as to how Wisdom was obtained.

'Good afternoon, Nate,' Alfred greeted me.

'Good afternoon, Alfred,' I replied.

'How are you doing today?' said Alfred, placing the cappuccino I had ordered earlier on my table.

'I'm fine, how about you?' I said.

'Energetic; it is a busy day after all.' Alfred looked at the entrance and said. 'Look at who just came.'

I looked at the entrance to see Plato, along with Protagoras, enter the café and walk toward us.

'Good afternoon, Alfred,' said Plato and Alfred greeted back.

I was so happy to see Plato coming and when Plato only greeted Alfred and said nothing to me, I felt sadness and I said to myself, 'If I sat with Plato two times before that doesn't mean we are now friends. He is a grown-up man, not a kid like me. I can't push myself into his world.' At that moment, I thought that the thing or person that gave me a purpose in life, the thing that I'd waited so long for, might just go away and that idea made me feel depressed and a little bit scared.

'Busy day, Alfred, isn't it?' said Protagoras.

'Yes, it is,' Alfred replied. 'I'm afraid there is not a single vacant table right now for you to sit at.'

'What do you mean, Alfred?' said Plato, pulling out a chair at my table. 'This is a table we are welcome at, right?'

I didn't expect Plato to say this and I replied gladly saying, 'Always!'

As Plato and Protagoras sat at my table, I felt a sense of relief from the emotions I'd built out of my wrong assumptions.

'How are you, son?' Plato said to me.

'I'm fine, how about you?' I replied.

'I'm doing great!' said Plato. 'Alfred, could you bring me the usual tea, please?'

'Right away, sir' Alfred replied and then left.

'Protagoras and I were just discussing something he read on Twitter,' said Plato.

'What is it about?' I asked.

'It is about Justice and Equality,' answered Protagoras.

'Don't worry, we just started,' said Plato. 'Could you read the twit again, Protagoras?'

'It is called a tweet,' said Protagoras with a smile.

'Don't bother correcting me,' said Plato. 'I can barely remember my name; just read the twit!'

Plato's last sentence made me smile.

'All right,' said Protagoras, gripping his smart phone and reading from it. 'The tweet reads as follows, "When all people are treated equally without any discrimination, this is Justice. When resources are distributed equally among the people, this is Justice. There can't be justice without Equality and wherever you see Equality implemented, you see Justice. This means that Justice is Equality and Equality is Justice." And that's the end of the tweet.'

'What do you think?' Plato asked me.

I hesitated at first and then answered, 'I think it is a correct statement.'

'What about you, Protagoras?' said Plato.

Protagoras turned his screen off, put his phone down on the table and said, 'To be honest, I never thought about this topic before. Therefore, I need to examine it first before making any judgment.'

'Of course,' replied Plato, 'I, too, never thought about it. Why don't we work together in examining it?'

I had also never thought about it before, but that didn't keep me from giving an answer. I got the feeling that both of Plato and Protagoras noticed that I didn't know what I was talking about and this made me feel embarrassed and I became a little bit introverted.

'Let's do it,' said Protagoras.

'Let us first identify the statement we want to examine,' said Plato.

'I believe the simplest statement we need to examine is whether Equality is Justice or not?' said Protagoras.

'I agree,' said Plato, 'and to do that we need to examine both Justice and Equality aside from each other and identify them.'

'That is a must,' replied Protagoras.

'Let us start then with Justice,' said Plato. 'What is Justice?'

Protagoras smiled at Plato for a while and said, 'If it was that simple, we wouldn't have to break it down, would we?'

Plato looked at me and said, 'I tried to take a shortcut, but he caught me.'

Seeing that Plato wanted to cheer me up, I knew that he noticed my withdrawal and I wanted to change that.

'There is no shortcut in those things,' I said with a smile, giving the impression that I was fully engaged even though I was a little introverted.

'You are also with him against me!' spoke Plato. 'I guess there is no other way.'

'No, there isn't,' said Protagoras with a smile.

'Well then, let's take it from the top,' Plato started speaking a little bit seriously. 'It is as you said, Protagoras, it is not simple to define Justice. As a matter of fact, I don't think there is a definition out there that has met my satisfaction.'

'I feel the same way,' said Protagoras.

'In that case, what should we do? Where should we start to understand or get the definition of Justice?' asked Plato.

'If we don't know what something is, knowing its features will help in identifying it,' answered Protagoras.

'That is the right approach,' said Plato. 'Why don't we start by asking ourselves, is justice related to every act or conduct?'

'Not all of them, but at least to the good ones,' replied Protagoras.

'Correct, and if someone is doing good acts, isn't he being just?' asked Plato.

'Yes, he is,' answered Protagoras.

'Let's look into this point further by examining an act and seeing how it relates to justice,' suggested Plato.

'Let's do it,' replied Protagoras.

'Let's take the act of generosity,' spoke Plato. 'For example, imagine there is a person who is not in need of money and you gave him some. How would you describe your act: is it generous, just, or both?'

Plato's example really intrigued me, and I was now very eager to see the logical conclusion of it.

'That is a very good and tough example, Plato,' started Protagoras, 'but before I answer you, I need to know one thing, is this act coming at the expense of someone else, someone who is in need of money, for example?'

'No, not at all. There are no hidden factors in the example, only the ones mentioned,' replied Plato.

'In this case,' Protagoras continued, 'I am sure the act is that of generosity, but I don't see justice or injustice related to it.'

'Let us take another example.' As Plato said this, I felt a little disappointed for I thought there would be some kind of a logical explanation or revelation behind the previous example and not just a prompt end. 'How would you describe the act of kindness towards strangers: is it kind, just, or both?'

'It can be both,' said Protagoras. 'It is kind for being kind and, as strangers have the right to be treated with kindness, it is just for keeping that right and not breaking it.'

Plato smiled and said, 'You have just brought up a good point, one that we'll have to skip for now and get back to it when the time is right. Now, going back to the example, I agree with what you've said, but what about if this stranger did you wrong—how would you describe your act of kindness towards him: kind, just, or both?'

'In this case, the act will be of kindness and that of forgiveness, mercy, or something similar,' said Protagoras, 'but it won't be an act of justice.'

'You are right. So, it seems that we have arrived to a point where justice has no relation, is that correct?' said Plato.

'It seems so,' replied Protagoras.

'And kindness is a good act, isn't it?' asked Plato.

'Of course it is,' answered Protagoras.

'Therefore, Justice is not related to every good act as we have assumed earlier?' said Plato.

'No, not necessarily,' replied Protagoras.

'Since we set out to find the features of Justice,' spoke Protagoras, 'we shouldn't stop here. We need to find out what is this part that Justice is not related to.'

'That we must indeed,' said Plato. 'What are Kindness, Generosity, and Mercy types of? What is their genre or field? I hope you understood me because I'm lacking a better word to describe what I mean.'

'I understood you,' said Protagoras. 'Kindness, Generosity, and so on, are different kinds of conduct, or better, manners that when a person is associated with any one of them, he will be characterized by it.'

'Very good, that is exactly what I meant. And what about Justice?' said Plato.

Protagoras replied with, 'Well, a lot of situations involve more than one kind of manners, right?'

'Correct,' replied Plato.

'And in some of those situations,' Protagoras continued, 'you would see Justice along with another kind of manners, like kindness or mercy. And so, in such situations, do we see Justice superior to the other kinds of manners or do we see Justice equivalent to it?'

'We see it equivalent to it,' said Plato. 'Neither is depending on the other for its existence.'

'Acts always involve, at least, one kind of manners, whether good or evil, and since Justice can be seen only in some acts and not all of them,' Protagoras continued, 'and since Justice is equivalent to other kinds of manners like Mercy and Kindness, therefore, Justice is a part of manners and not above it. Thus, it is a kind of manners.'

'Well put, Protagoras!' said Plato. 'Being just is only a kind of manners that some people are characterized by while others are not.'

Now I understood the reason behind Plato's examples. He chose qualities that could stand independent from, and were as strong as, Justice itself. It was all to deduce on the nature of Justice and its relation to manners.

'I'm glad that we've identified one feature of Justice,' said Protagoras, 'but I don't see myself drawn yet to a clear definition of what Justice is.'

'In that case,' spoke Plato, 'we should continue investigating more features about Justice.'

'That we must,' replied Protagoras.

'What is Justice associated with?' asked Plato.

'For sure, Justice is associated with laws and rights,' answered Protagoras.

'What are laws and rights?' asked Plato.

'Rights are things a person should have as a human, firstly, and as part of a society, secondly,' answered Protagoras. 'Like the right to speak, mobility, shelter, food, practice traditions, and so on, as long as they don't harm other people.'

'Very good, and what about laws?' said Plato.

'Laws are enforceable rules of conduct set by an authority that can be met with punishment if not followed.' Protagoras continued, 'like traffic laws, criminal laws, environmental laws and so on.'

'Good, and how is Justice associated with rights and laws?' said Plato.

'By sustaining them and restoring them if they are ever broken,' replied Protagoras.

'So, when someone is doing an act that helps in keeping a right or a law, is he being just?' said Plato.

'Correct,' Protagoras replied.

Plato continued, 'And when someone is doing an act that restores a right or a law, is he being just?'

'Correct,' replied Protagoras.

'Sustaining a right is not the same as restoring it, is it?' asked Plato.

'No, it is not,' answered Protagoras.

'Could one act have two different actions?' said Plato.

'A word can have multiple meanings, but one meaning cannot have more than one connotation or significance.'

'Exactly,' said Plato. 'Then, how could Justice be used for both sustaining and restoring rights and laws?'

'It shouldn't be. We must be missing something here,' said Protagoras, gripping his chin by his thumb and index finger, lost in his thoughts.

After a while, Plato spoke saying, 'Let me ask you this, when Justice is implemented, is it in post-crime or pre-crime situations?'

'How do you define crime here?' asked Protagoras.

'The breaking of laws and the disposition of rights,' answered Plato.

Protagoras stayed silent for a while in his thoughts, until Plato broke that silence with, 'Where do we see justice being implemented?'

'In the court of law or the court of justice, hence the name,' replied Protagoras. 'That is, of course, officially. Justice can be seen implemented anywhere.'

'That is correct,' said Plato, 'and when it happens in the court, is it pre-crime or post-crime?'

'It is, of course, post-crime,' replied Protagoras.

'What about pre-crime?' said Plato. 'Can justice be implemented, officially, pre-crime outside the court?'

'You can prevent a crime that is about to happen but hasn't happened yet,' said Protagoras. 'But I don't think you can implement justice and judge people who haven't committed any crime.'

'So now, we see justice only involved or associated with post-crime matters, isn't that right?' said Plato.

'It seems that way,' replied Protagoras.

'Before we continue,' said Plato, 'why don't we summarize what we have arrived to so far about Justice. Nate, can you do that?'

'Sure,' I said, caught between taking a moment to think things over and taking too long to answer and hoping that I didn't forget anything. 'We said that Justice is a kind of manners. Also, it's related to rights and laws in… situations that are… happening after the crime has already happened.'

'Very good, Nate!' said Plato. 'Now, what do you think we should question next about Justice?'

Plato's request took me by surprise. It was not that I wasn't focusing on the conversation, it was that I wasn't expected to speak or say anything and so I replied, stammering, 'What about… what does Justice do?'

'Excellent question! One that we should tackle, Protagoras,' said Plato.

'Indeed,' replied Protagoras.

I was so relieved that he directed the question towards Protagoras and didn't want to examine it with me.

'Our question here will be,' spoke Plato, 'what is the function of Justice?'

Protagoras replied saying, 'Since Justice is associated with laws and rights, and since it is associated with the breaking of those laws and rights in a post-crime situation, therefore, it is only fitting to say that the function of Justice is to restore laws and rights to their respective places or people.'

'Very sound,' said Plato. 'It is just as you described it earlier.'

Upon hearing this I said to myself, 'Very good, Nate, you asked a question that has already been answered; what an idiot!' I was really trying to add to the conversation and not be a drag, but it wasn't easy. I guess the art of speaking wasn't that simple.

'Not quite,' spoke Protagoras. 'Earlier, I added sustainability, which is a pre-crime matter, but we came to the conclusion that Justice isn't associated with rights and laws in pre-crime matters.'

'That is true, which means that we shouldn't stop here while we have many things left to examine and figure out,' said Plato.

This is something I had come to love about the conversations with Plato and his friends. Things were never what they seemed to be in the beginning and each topic brought other issues that were related to it.

'What other things?' asked Protagoras.

Plato then extended his arm and reached out to the sugar sachet holder on the table and picked up two white sugar sachets and a brown one. He then started arranging them on the table. He put the brown sachet horizontally first, and then positioned one white sachet perpendicular to the brown sachet in the lower side, and positioned the other sachet diagonally in the upper side of the brown sachet.

Plato said, 'The white sugar sachets represent the situations rights and laws are in while the brown sachet divides the states of pre-crime and post-crime, the lower part and the upper part respectively. In the pre-crime side, rights and laws are being followed whilst in the post-crime side, they have been broken and are being violated.'

Plato then took a wooden stirring stick and broke off four small pieces. He then placed two pieces on the white sachets, one on each, and placed one piece next to each of the sachets as well. Plato spoke and numbered the pieces as he placed them from one to four.

'In each side, there are two possible actions involving rights and laws— or let's just refer to them only by rights for a smoother talk.' Plato continued, 'Those actions are represented in the diagram by the wooden pieces bringing the total to four actions.'

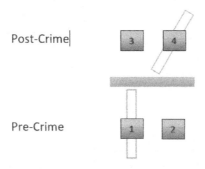

'What are those four actions?' said Protagoras

'In the pre-crime status,' Plato continued, 'rights are in a state of being followed and implemented which leaves us with only two possible actions that can be done with rights here: either sustaining and keeping them or breaking them.

'On the other side of the post-crime status, rights are in the state of being disregarded and violated, leaving only two possible actions to be done here: either restoring rights, symbolized by making the white sachet straight and aligned again with the other white sachet, or continue violating them.'

'That is correct,' said Protagoras.

'We agreed earlier that one act or meaning cannot have more than one action, correct?' asked Plato.

'Correct,' replied Protagoras.

'And if we want to truly know something, such as Justice,' said Plato, 'we need to know its boundaries and, not only that, we need to know the topics closely associated with it.'

'That is essential,' said Protagoras.

'Therefore, we need to find out the names of the four possible actions concerning rights,' said Plato.

'We already know that the act of restoring rights is called "Justice",' said Protagoras. 'We only need to know the names of the three remaining actions.'

'That is correct,' spoke Plato. 'Our actions again are as follows: action one for sustaining rights, action two for breaking rights, action three for restoring rights, which is named Justice, action four for continuing violating rights. Let's take each action, one by one, and see what its proper name is.'

I never thought that a discussion about Justice would reach this extent. I was very excited with this diagrammatical example and I was very enthusiastic to know what those three actions beside justice were.

'Let's start with the first action: sustaining rights.' Plato continued, 'When you are following the law and keeping every right in its proper place, whether while treating people, animals, or inanimated objects, how would you describe your actions?'

'I would say that I am being fair,' replied Protagoras.

Plato replied with, 'So you think the name of the action is fairness, right?'

'I believe equity is a more fitting name here,' said Protagoras.

'What is equity?' asked Plato.

'Equity is the act of treating everything and everyone rightly, fairly, and impartially,' answered Protagoras. 'Equity is giving or keeping everyone's rights without shortage or excess at the expense of others.'

'Fair enough, so to speak,' said Plato, smiling. 'Let's move on to the second action which includes acts that involve the breaking of laws and the violation of rights. Acts that comprise taking rights from their respective places either displacing them or straight pillaging them from others. What do you call, or how would you describe, such actions?'

'Taking others' rights from them is a tyrannical act,' said Protagoras. 'Therefore, I think the name of the action here will be Tyranny.'

'Tyranny here is a fitting choice and I think you explained it well,' said Plato.

'The third action in our diagrammatical example is Justice as we agreed earlier,' spoke Protagoras. 'We can summarize Justice as restoring violated rights to their rightful owners fairly without extent or scarcity and delivering punishment in the same manner as well.'

'Well said, Professor,' spoke Plato. 'Let us move then to the fourth and last action, which is the continuation of desecrating already violated acts. How would you describe actions that involve fighting justice from being implemented or preventing someone from restoring his stolen or taken rights?'

Protagoras replied, 'The act or process of continuing to violate rights and suppress any attempt of restoring them to their respective owners is called Oppression.'

'I agree with that,' said Plato. 'It seems we have arrived to all of the four actions associated with rights.'

'It seems that way,' said Protagoras. 'They are as follows: first action, Equity, for sustaining rights; second action, Tyranny, for breaking rights; third action, Justice, for restoring rights; fourth action, Oppression, for continuously violating rights.'

'Do you see any angle we haven't covered regarding this approach?' said Plato.

'No, I think we covered everything,' replied Protagoras.

I really liked the conclusions or answers that Plato's diagram brought; they were really insightful, easy to follow, and understand.

'With what we know about Justice so far, do you think we can give a definition to it?' asked Plato.

'I think we can,' answered Protagoras.

'Great! Let's hear it,' requested Plato.

'Justice is the act of restoring rights to their rightful places and owners without excess or shortage to what a person deserves. And the same manner will go to the person who is receiving the punishment.'

'I agree with what you said about restoring rights,' spoke Plato, 'but I don't think the same goes for delivering punishments.'

'Why is that?' said Protagoras.

'Because restoring something and delivering something aren't the same thing and they go against what we agreed earlier on regarding the idea that meanings can't have multiple significances.' Plato continued, 'When it comes to giving punishment to a culprit, the punishment has to be fair in regard to the crime committed. If the punishment was too much, we would be committing a tyrannical act against the culprit. On the other hand, if the punishment was too little, we would be committing a tyrannical act against the victim, even if his rights were restored. Thus, when it comes to delivering punishment, I see Equity is the more fitting choice here than Justice.'

Protagoras thought for a moment and said, 'I agree with you. This leaves the definition of Justice with only restoring rights.'

'Very good, Protagoras,' said Plato as he started to put the sugar sachets back in the holder. 'It seems we have arrived to what we set out to find initially.'

'What do you mean?' asked Protagoras, confused.

'We have found the definition of Justice,' replied Plato, 'or at least we found a satisfying answer to what Justice is.'

'Correct, but that is not what we sat out to find originally,' said Protagoras. 'We wanted to see whether Equality is Justice or not.'

Plato stayed silent for a moment then said, 'Oh yeah, I totally forgot!' He started laughing gently and Protagoras followed him with laughter.

I couldn't help but laugh with them as well for I, too, had forgotten about Equality. It was a refreshing moment to see Plato and Protagoras outside their serious conversational atmosphere.

'Is Equality Justice or not?' said Plato.

'I think we should go with the same examination manner we used in Justice,' said Protagoras.

'Wait a second, I think I have something that can help us with our examination,' said Plato, grabbing his smart phone and typing on it. 'Look at these two images.' Plato showed us the images on his phone. 'On both images, we see three people with different heights: a tall person, a short person, and an average-height person, all trying to watch a game from behind the tall fence.' Plato continued, 'In the left image, we see the three people have been given one box each. They have all been treated equally, but that doesn't mean they have been treated justly. Let us examine how each of the three persons has been treated.

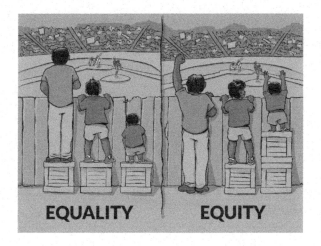

'The tall person has been given a box which he doesn't need to see past the fence, as he is taller than the fence. How would you describe the treatment he received, Nate?'

'I would say that he was treated with generosity,' I said, little hesitant. 'But knowing that this generosity came on the expense of the short person I would say that the act itself is that of tyranny, because a right has been taken from a more deserving person.'

'Very good!' said Plato. 'And how would you describe the treatment the average-height person received?'

'It will be Equity, each person got exactly what he needs, no more or less,' I replied.

'Good, and what about the short person?' said Plato.

'He was treated with tyranny,' I said. 'He received less than what he needed, and so he didn't receive his full right.'

'Excellent! What about the right image, how would you say the three people were treated?' said Plato.

'They were treated with Equity, of course,' I replied.

'Very good,' said Plato. 'Going back to the left image, if we took the box from the tall person and gave it to the short person, how would you say each of the two persons were treated?'

I thought about the question for a moment and then answered. 'Regarding the short person, I'd say he was treated justly since his right was restored to him. As for the tall person, I'd say he was treated fairly or with Equity.'

'What do you think, Protagoras?' asked Plato.

'I think Nate has said it appropriately,' replied Protagoras.

When Plato asked Protagoras what he thought of my answer, I felt that I must have messed up and that Plato wasn't satisfied with my answer. Even though Protagoras agreed with me, I still left a feeling of insecurity.

'So, regarding the manner of distributing boxes on both images, how would you describe it?' said Plato, directing his question towards Protagoras.

'Equally in the left image and unequally in the right one,' said Protagoras.

'So, equality on the left and inequality on the right?' said Plato.

'That's right,' replied Protagoras.

'What were the outcomes when the three people were treated equally?' said Plato.

'Equity and Tyranny,' replied Protagoras.

Plato continued, 'And, hypothetically, if the tall person was given two boxes and the average-height person one box, while the short person none, wouldn't this be an example of an unequal distribution of boxes?'

'Yes, it would be,' replied Protagoras.

'What would be the outcomes of this inequality?' asked Plato.

'Equity and Tyranny,' answered Protagoras.

'We see both equality and inequality have resulted in more than one form of treatment, don't we?' said Plato.

'Yes, we do,' replied Protagoras.

'Therefore, Equality doesn't necessarily mean Equity or Tyranny,' spoke Plato, 'but instead, it can result in both depending on the circumstances?'

'Yes, it does,' replied Protagoras.

'All of our examples regarding Equality and Inequality have been in the pre-crime state,' said Plato. 'Let's apply them to the post-crime state. Let's assume a second hypothetical situation where the tall person has two boxes, the average-height person with no box, and the short person with one box. Using our second hypothetical example of unequal distribution and applying Equality to it, where we will be taking one box from the tall person and giving it to the average-height person, what outcome will we get?'

'The average-height person will be served Justice while the short person will be treated with oppression as his right will continue to be violated,' said Protagoras.

'Correct, and what outcomes did equality result in in this post-crime state?' asked Plato.

'Both Justice and Oppression,' answered Protagoras. 'And there is no doubt that the application of inequality in a post-crime state will result in both Justice and Oppression.'

'Correct,' spoke Plato. 'At the end, we see that both Equality and Inequality can result in any of the four actions; Equity, Tyranny, Justice, and Oppression, meaning neither one is solely related to or is associated exclusively with any of them.'

'You are absolutely right, Plato,' said Protagoras. 'This way, our question of "Is Equality Justice?" has been answered.'

'Before wc go into that, we must define both Equality and Inequality,' spoke Plato. 'Because all we have done so far is speak about their applications and the outcomes they result in.'

'Fair enough,' spoke Protagoras. 'Equality is the manner of treating others impartially, likely and with equivalence. While Inequality will be the opposite.'

'I don't see any fault in that,' said Plato. 'Now, going back to the original statement in the twit, "Equality is Justice": is this a correct statement or not?'

I smiled upon hearing Plato mispronouncing the name of a tweet yet again.

'It is a false statement as we have just seen that Equality can result in multiple things,' said Protagoras. 'And a thing that is associated with more than one thing, can't mean definitively any of them.'

'You are correct, but why is that?' said Plato.

'What do you mean?' replied Protagoras.

'Why is it that Equality is associated with more than one thing instead of only one?' said Plato.

'I don't quite understand what you mean?' said Protagoras.

'Look at it this way,' spoke Plato. 'Equality and its opposite, are by nature a manner of conduct not an application of Justice or any other specific subject. Therefore, they can result in many things while not meaning any of them exclusively as we agreed earlier.

'Equality and Inequality are not limited to our example of rights and laws, but they can extend to all sorts of topics as they are, in the end, only a form of treatment. They are not particularly good or bad by themselves, it depends entirely on their applications and the results they bring, which can be either good or bad.

'Going back to the statement of "Equality is Justice", as per our discussion, this is a false judgment and a misleading statement. The former is a general manner of conduct while the latter is a specific action. And when it comes to how you should treat others, since Equality can result in a bad manner, it is more suitable to aim for Equity and Justice, for they always carry good results.'

'Well said! As always, Plato,' complimented Protagoras.

At this moment, I withdrew into my mind, blocking Plato's and Protagoras' voices so all I could hear was the faint mumbling of the crowd, the tinkling of the tableware that filled the air, and the classical music that was playing. I was reflecting on today's topic and the result we reached. It was really fascinating how words with only thin differences could have big differential meanings. I had never given words with similar seeming meanings any deep attention as to what they really meant and I had always used them interchangeably. The conversation opened my eyes to the wide possibilities of words and their meanings and that I should know exactly what a word means before using it.

But more importantly, I was reflecting on my performance in the discussion and how bad it was. I had spoken without giving thoughts to my words, saying things I didn't believe in, and asking questions that had already been answered. I was unreliable to the conversation and I felt that Plato and Protagoras believed so as well. To be honest, I had thought I would do better than this and now I was upset with myself, and so, for the rest of the time I sat with Plato and Protagoras, I remained silent, thinking about whether I could ever become like them—a person who could speak wisely.

CHAPTER 4

Right and Wrong

A few days later, I came with Plato to the café.

'Good afternoon, Plato,' greeted Alfred as we entered the café.

'Good afternoon, Alfred,' replied Plato. 'How are you doing today?'

'Splendid!' said Alfred. 'Your group is sitting at the back of the café, next to your favorite fresco.'

'Next to the "School Of Athens". I love sitting there,' said Plato. 'Thank you, Alfred.'

'My pleasure,' replied Alfred.

After that, Plato and I started walking to the back of the café.

'Can I ask you one question, Plato?' I said.

'Sure, you can ask me anything,' replied Plato.

'What do you do for living?' I asked.

'I worked in the education system where first I was a teacher and then I became a school principal,' answered Plato. 'Now, I am retired.'

'What subject did you teach?' I asked.

'I taught social studies and I loved every minute of it,' answered Plato.

'It sounds like your kind of subject,' I said. 'What did you love about it so much?'

'As the topics I taught can relate to real life, I loved going off script and just talking to students about real-life matters,' said Plato.

'Knowing your speaking style, I'll bet your students loved you,' I said.

Later, we reached the end of the café and found Luqman and Hypatia sitting at a table with two sofas and an armchair. We exchanged greetings with them and joined their table.

'How are you, Nate?' said Hypatia, who was dressed in a casual way.

'I'm fine, and you?' I replied.

'Great!' Hypatia replied.

'Please continue what you were discussing,' said Plato. 'We would love to hear your discussion.'

'We weren't discussing any topic,' said Luqman.

'How do you find the topics discussed in the group so far, Nate?' asked Hypatia.

'Very insightful and interesting,' I replied.

'If I'm not mistaken,' spoke Plato, 'you want to have a conversation with Nate, don't you, Hypatia?'

'Was I that obvious?' said Hypatia. 'Anyway, what do you think Nate, are you up to it?'

'Anyway, Nate, it is a sweet little topic that I think you'd love. What do you think? If you're up to it, it would be great. If you're not, no worries, I can discuss it with either Plato or Luqman.'

I thought about it for a moment. The only way to get over a fear is to face it. It would be a great opportunity to engage in a discussion and ger rid of the insecurities I still felt from the last discussion with Plato and Protagoras. Besides, a sweet little discussion might be exactly what I needed.

'I'll do my best, but don't expect the same level of conversation as you guys have,' I replied.

'Your best is good,' said Hypatia.

Alfred served us a pot of tea and Plato started pouring for the both of us. Right then, my hands started shaking a bit, I wasn't sure why—was it fear, was it excitement, or a little bit of both? I really wanted to test myself in a conversation, but I guess adrenaline shoots up when you're doing things you're not used to yet.

'Tell me, Nate,' started Hypatia, 'if there were no prophets or messengers sent and if there were no holy books, how are right and wrong determined?'

I chuckled inside my head. *She said it was sweet and little.*

'That's an interesting topic,' commented Plato.

For a moment, I thought about what would I do If I was ever put in a situation where what is right wasn't known to me and said, 'I think by instinct and feelings. Sometimes, when facing a situation where I don't know what is the right way to act, I act based on my instinct and feelings and it turns out to be the right thing to do.'

'I don't know you well, Nate,' said Hypatia, 'but I assume that you are a part of a well-raised and well-educated family, right?'

'Why would you assume that?' I asked.

'Because of what I've seen from you so far,' Hypatia started answering. 'You speak politely, your hair is neat, and you are dressed fashionably. I've seen you wearing beautiful T-Shirts and jeans that work perfectly with each other. It is as if you have an older sister that checks your taste on clothing and gives her advice when needed.'

'I assume that you took care of your little brother's and sisters' fashion, am I right?' said Plato.

'You have no Idea!' said Hypatia. 'When I was young, I was an evil fashion dictator. I would put my nose in anything fashion-related.'

'You must have had a big Barbie doll collection when you were young, right?' said Luqman.

'Not a single one,' said Hypatia. 'Back then, I used my little brother as a dress-up and I put him in the full package: dress, make-up and all.'

'What have you done?' said Plato with a smile.

Hypatia chuckled and said, 'My little brother didn't mind it back then. Every time I would dress him up, he would go to our mother and show her how beautiful he looks.' Plato and Luqman laughed, as did I. 'Anyway, how is my deduction of you, Nate, is it true?'

'Well… you got one part wrong: I don't have an elder sister dictating my fashion. I'm the eldest son; I have a younger sister and a brother,' I said, happy of the details that Hypatia noticed about me. 'And the reason I dress this way is that I like to appear representable to people.'

'But generally, you do come from a well-raised and a well-educated family, right?' said Hypatia.

'You could say that, I guess,' I replied.

'Going back to our conversation now, I see you as a good and honest person and because of that,' said Hypatia, 'when you rely on your instinct and feelings, you're most probably going to do the right thing. But, there is an important thing you need to consider, not everyone shares your values and what might seem right or wrong to you might seem the opposite to someone else, right?

'Yes, that is true,' I said.

'Do people have the same instinct or do they differ with each individual?' asked Hypatia.

'They of course differ,' I answered.

'And so, each of them will have his own judgement of what is right and what is wrong, is that correct?' said Hypatia.

'Correct,' I replied.

'Will those judgments always agree with each other or might they sometimes agree and at other times disagree?' said Hypatia.

'They will agree and disagree,' I replied.

'So then, can we use instinct to determine what's right and what's wrong?' said Hypatia.

'No, we can't,' I replied.

'What about feelings?' asked Hypatia.

'It goes without saying that feelings will have the same argument as instinct,' I answered. 'People feel differently about what's right and what's wrong.'

'You are right,' said Hypatia. 'With instinct and feeling out of the picture, how are right and wrong determined then?'

'What about pain?' I suggested. 'People might have different instincts and feelings, but surely they can all agree on what is painful and what is not. This way, anything that causes pain must be wrong, and anything that causes pleasure must be right, correct?'

'Tell me then,' said Hypatia, 'when you give a child a syringe shot or when you fix a broken limb of a person, don't you do that for their own good?'

'Yes,' I replied.

'During the procedure, do they feel pain or pleasure by your action?' said Hypatia.

'They feel pain,' I replied.

'Since they felt pain, you must have performed the wrong thing then, right?' said Hypatia.

'Quite the opposite,' I replied.

'Even though it causes pain?' said Hypatia.

'It is true that they felt pain at the beginning,' I said, 'but at the end, a person with a broken limb will feel pleasure for getting his limp fixed or at least for making the pain go away, as well with a sick child.'

'So, a painful act is considered right as long as it takes away pain or causes pleasure at the end?' said Hypatia.

'Correct,' I replied.

'I think you might need to rephrase your previous statement of how right and wrong are determined,' said Hypatia.

I gathered my thoughts and said, 'The end result feeling of pain or pleasure determines what's right and wrong.'

'What is the desired end result feeling of your statement?' said Hypatia.

'Pleasure or the removal of pain,' I said.

'Let me ask you this,' said Hypatia, 'crying out of sorrow and grief, does it cause pain or pleasure?'

'Pain, of course,' I replied.

'And when you lose someone dear to you, or go through anything that causes a similar emotional impact on you,' Hypatia continued, 'is it better to keep it inside of you and never cry it out or is it better to cry and let it out?'

'It's better to cry it out for sure,' I replied. 'Keeping such a thing inside of you surely has some health and psychological effects.'

'In this case,' said Hypatia, 'feeling pain is the right thing to do and avoiding it is the wrong thing, am I correct?'

'You are correct, because at the end, the caused pain, crying, will stop and the original pain, sorrow, will go away. So, this makes it a way to relieve one from pain, thus making it right.'

'What you're talking about here is the middle normal state,' said Hypatia.

'What do you mean?' I said.

'Aren't pleasure and pain contrary to each other?' said Hypatia.

'Yes, they are,' I replied.

Hypatia continued, 'And isn't there a point in between the two where one doesn't feel either of them or might be feeling both of them depending on how you look at it?'

'I guess so,' I replied.

Hypatia continued, 'And isn't this the point you meant in the previous example when you spoke about taking away pain, which is to bring one from pain to the midpoint where he isn't feeling pleasure but he is not at pain any longer?'

'That is correct,' I replied.

Hypatia continued, 'Tell me, when people feel pleasure, do they stay pleasant all the time until something painful happens to them or do they go back to the normal state, the midpoint between pain and pleasure?'

'Of course, they don't stay pleasant all the time,' I said. 'They go back to the normal state even without something painful happening to them.'

'If I recall correctly, you called the movement from the state of pain to normal a right thing, correct?' said Hypatia.

'Yes,' I replied.

'What about the movement from pleasure to the normal state, is it right or wrong?' said Hypatia.

'Well, according to my logic, it should be wrong,' I said, 'but it doesn't feel right to say that. Pleasure doesn't last and it is only normal for it to disappear after it has lasted its time.'

'You are absolutely correct,' said Hypatia, 'it is normal for pleasure to go away, just as it is normal for pain to go away. Thus, this movement we're speaking about can't be a determinant of what is right and what is wrong.'

'I agree,' I said, 'so, we are left with only that which causes pleasure to determine what's right and wrong.'

'Then we shall examine it,' spoke Hypatia. 'Don't people feel pleasure when they take some drugs?'

'Yes, they do,' I replied.

'Is what they are doing right or wrong?' said Hypatia.

'It is surely wrong because it will harm them,' I replied.

'And don't we see some people who find pleasure in dishonorable things like murder, rape, unfaithfulness, bribery, and so on?' said Hypatia.

'Yes, there are people like this,' I said.

'Do you consider what they find pleasure in, right or wrong?' asked Hypatia.

'Of course, I find it wrong,' I answered.

'Therefore, pleasure can't be a determinant of what's right and wrong and neither is pain,' said Hypatia. 'People differ with what they find dolorous and pleasant. Some things are perceived painful to some and pleasant to others. For this reason, personal elements can't be used to determine right and wrong. We need to look into something else.'

'That is correct,' I said. 'If a person can't determine what is right and what is wrong all by himself, what about the people? Can't what they perceive be used as a determinant?'

'I see what you mean,' said Hypatia. 'People don't think the same and they will surely have some contradictory opinions. If such a case happens and one thing was found right by one group and wrong by the other group, what should we do then?'

'In this case, the right thing will be determined by the majority,' I said.

'And how is the majority?' said Hypatia.

'What do you mean?' I replied.

'How do you find the majority of people of our time?' Hypatia started. 'Do you find them intelligent or ignorant, generous or selfish, pious or materialistic, honorable or shameful, courageous or unfaithful, and lastly, with virtue or with vice?'

'To be honest,' I said, 'it is true that there are a lot of people with the positive traits that you just mentioned, but I find the majority to be on the negative side.'

'What about men of antiquity?' Hypatia continued. 'The prophets of the lord, who came to raise human affairs beyond that which is tangible and ending, to that which is felt, understood and everlasting—weren't they faced with heresy, blasphemy, and sacrilege by the materialistic majority?

'And what about the philosophers of ancient time, who asked men to pursue honorable things in life like knowledge, wisdom, and virtue instead of striving after lust and desires— weren't they fought against and even murdered by the immodest majority? And what about the polymaths of old, whose knowledge and ideas were ahead of their time and who wanted to advance civilization to its best—weren't they ignored, ridiculed, and silenced by the ignorant majority?

'And if history has proven anything, it is that the majority never was right. All of the great things in life like wisdom, knowledge, and virtues have always had few audiences and even lesser initiates. All of those things don't come easily; they require strong heart, will, determination and an even stronger patience to be earned. Most people choose the easy path in life, the path of worldly lust and desire, and they run away from the virtuous path, if they ever knew of its existence in the first place. Those who do find it and walk in it are few in number and those among them who actually walk the path to its end are even fewer.

'Take slavery as an example. Wasn't there a period of time in different parts of the world where the trading of slaves was considered as a good thing and not an evil act? This, of course, lasted until a minority stood against the multitude and fought for the rights of slaves and helped bring an end to slavery and, not only that, they helped issue some punishment against such act as well.

'If we ever take our moral principles from the majority, righteousness will surely be lost and its identity will be worn by falseness masquerading as righteousness. Do you see now, my dear Nate, why the majority can't ever be a determinant of right and wrong?'

'Before you answer, Nate,' interrupted Plato, 'I have to say, that was beautiful, Hypatia!'

'I also agree with that,' said Luqman.

Hypatia smiled and thanked Plato.

'I agree with your statement, Hypatia,' I said.

'Then, we need to find a new determinant beside the majority,' said Hypatia.

I replied with, 'What about the law? Can it be used as a determinant?'

'Why did you choose the law?' asked Hypatia.

'Because laws are chosen by the supreme court,' I answered, 'which consists of more than one highly-intelligent, highly-educated person, a group who combines their minds together to create the laws. This way, an individual's perspective won't be the base of what is right and wrong and it won't be done by the majority, but instead, by the collective knowledge and experience of the people in the court.'

'Let me ask you this, what are the principles that the laws are based and decided on?' said Hypatia.

'I didn't understand you,' I replied.

'When the supreme court gathers together to set up, redefine, or remove a law,' said Hypatia, 'to whose favor will they be guided?'

'I think it depends on the type of rulership in the nation,' I said. 'In a dictatorship, the laws will be set to favor the ruler, but in a democracy, the laws will be set to favor the citizens.'

'Very good, let's examine both scenarios,' spoke Hypatia. 'In a dictatorship, don't you see laws that are unfair to the citizens in either monetary or humanistic ways? When we examine history, don't we see rulers that have enslaved nations through debt and have even declared some ethnicities to be lower than others to justify certain cruel acts to be bestowed upon them? The examples of such monstrous laws are plenty, so merely by being laws, does that mean they are right?'

'Of course, not,' I replied.

'Let's examine the laws made under democracy.' Hypatia continued, 'At the surface, laws made under a democratic rule will be centered around the benefit of the citizens, ensuring them their humanistic rights. While this is fine at the beginning, we must not neglect its furthest corners and its open development. For example, a court may see fit to neglect the help of other people or nations—as in foreign aid or refugees—for the benefit of their own people. They may see it is not wise to share their resources with others and keep them for their own citizens instead.

'We must not also forget the potential development of laws in democracy. At the end, democratic rule follows what the citizens want, and if it ever goes against what the people demand, it will be put under scrutiny and that might lead to the creation of some laws that were seen before as inhumane, to be justified for the satisfaction of the citizens. I'm not speaking here about obvious crimes like murder, rape, and so on. I'm speaking about things like unnecessary abortion and pedophilia. It is sad to see some great nations beginning to justify such cruel acts under the name of democracy. We must not also forget that democratic laws can be driven by the majority and if the intelligent minority ever stood against such laws, they will be ridiculed and titled with whatever 'isms' are going on in the world.

'After our examination, do you see the laws made by people as a trustworthy determinant of what is right and what is wrong?'

'As a matter of fact, I don't,' I said. 'I see a lot of immoral acts today justified just for being legal and, personally, I don't agree with their justification. Also, I don't see myself only with this stand. A lot of people cling to their traditions for their moral standards. And so if laws can't be the determinant of what is right and wrong, what about culture and traditions?

'The moral principles of right and wrong determined under cultural influence are not affected by what the law says. They are affected mainly by the people themselves and what they see fit. Could culture be the determinant we are looking for all this time?'

'You know, kiddo, if you had asked me this question twenty years ago I would've said yes,' spoke Hypatia. 'Back then everything was different. Life was simpler, people were satisfied with what little they had, manners were put ahead of fortune.' Hypatia then stayed silent for a moment and said, 'Now, seeing how the culture has changed so drastically for the worse, I can't say it can be used as a determinant of right and wrong.

'I remember in those days I had funny sleeping times. You see, when I was in kindergarten, I was forced to go to bed at 8pm. When I was in elementary school, it was 9pm. When I went to middle school, I could stay up until 10pm. And when I reached high school, I could stay up till I felt like sleeping. All those years, I had envied my big brother and sister, as I thought they could stay up all they wanted. Of course, at that time when they were forced to go to bed, I was already asleep and so I didn't realize they had bed times as well.'

'I remember this one time during a summer vacation,' Luqman started speaking, 'my parents had traveled and so I had to stay at my grandmother's house, no matter how grown up I told her I was, I was in high school back then, she would never allow me to stay home alone. And the thing about my grandmother is, she considered 9 pm to be very late and so she used to lock all of the house doors at that time. No one was allowed to leave after 9. If you were outside before 9, it was fine with her but leaving after noooo!

'And one night, while I was sleeping there, my high school friends wanted to go out after 9 and they asked me to come along. I didn't know what to say to them; I tried some lame excuses but they didn't buy them. And at last, I had to tell them that I was locked in and forbidden to leave. To this day, they laugh at me when that story gets mentioned.'

Hypatia laughed and said, 'But you could've gone out with your friends before 9 and then came back way later at night; why didn't you do that?'

'It is true that I could've done that,' Luqman replied, 'but then my grandmother would've stayed up all night till I came back. She wouldn't stay up to punish me, but with me outside, she couldn't sleep. She would stay worried until I came back. So, I couldn't go out with my friends having fun while I knew that she was worrying back home.'

'Back then,' Plato said, 'my mother needed to know the family of each friend I had. She wouldn't allow me to befriend a boy without knowing who he was and who his family was. One time I asked her why, and she said it was to keep me safe from ill-mannered boys.'

'My mother used to do the same,' spoke Luqman. 'I wasn't allowed to play with other kids in the street. She used to say that children neglected by their parents are thrown into the street to raise them, but you have a family that cares about you, why do you want to go to the street?'

Plato chuckled and said, 'it is unbelievable how traditions can change drastically in a few decades.'

'And it can get a little sad to see good ones get abandoned and replaced by inferior ones,' said Luqman. 'Where I come from, the Arabic culture, family is the top priority for any individual. It still is, but slowly its value is beginning to fade away as people get lost in life and its distractions. Back in the day when I was just a boy, family meant everything, and I don't mean just the small family, I mean the grand one with your grandparents, uncles, aunts, cousins, and so on. My family used to gather at my grandparents' house every Sunday night. I used to see my uncles, aunts, and cousins every week and not only during the holidays. My cousin was my best friend. The things we would do back then—I don't recall a gathering without us getting grounded by my grandfather.'

'A lot of families used to do the same thing when I was child,' said Plato. 'Now, some families only gather on the holidays, and some don't as they decide to spend it with their friends instead.' Plato let out a sad sigh and said, "Let us get back to the conversation.'

'Of course, of course,' said Hypatia. 'Now, Nate, where were we?'

'I asked you if culture and traditions can be used as a determinant of what is right and what is wrong?' I replied.

'Oh, right.' Hypatia was silent for a moment then continued, 'I had an argument in my mind, but then we started speaking about our stories and now I don't remember what I was going to say.'

'We can skip it, anyway. I am convinced that culture can't be used as a determinant,' I said.

'Convinced? How?' asked Hypatia.

I answered, 'After hearing your stories and seeing that when I sit with my grandfather he would tell the same kind of stories to me, I see how culture and traditions change along the years and not necessarily for the better.'

'Yes,' said Plato.

'Listen, Nate,' spoke Hypatia, 'we keep going in circles without going anywhere. We need to stop looking for the determinant in people for they always have many different and opposing moral principles which will bring us only to subjective results. The problem with subjectivity is that every possibility is acceptable: there is no right or wrong and this will render the determinant of what's right and wrong obsolete. Thus, we need to think in an objective manner.'

'I agree, but how do we do that?' I said.

'If we don't know the determinant, let us see which features ought to be in it,' said Hypatia.

'That sounds right,' I replied.

Hypatia said, 'Since we associated what is right with objectivity, it has to be only one thing and not many, in each particular topic or circumstance, right?

'Yes,' I replied.

Hypatia continued, 'And what is right has to be always the same and never changing, right?

'Correct,' I replied.

Hypatia continued, 'And what is morally right should always lead to virtues and not vices, right?'

'That's what should be,' I replied.

'These are all of the features that I could come up with,' spoke Hypatia. 'Do you have something to add?'

I thought for a second and replied with, 'Nothing comes to my mind.'

'Okay, so what kind of method or rule would help us determine what's right and wrong based on the features that we just agreed upon?' said Hypatia.

'What about right is what is beneficial?' I said. 'Thus, any action that would bring benefit to you will be right and any action that doesn't will be wrong.'

'Then, tell me,' said Hypatia, 'is stealing right or wrong?'

'Of course, it is wrong,' I replied.

Hypatia replied, 'But based on your rule, it should be right. Wouldn't stealing bring benefit to you?'

'That is correct,' I said, 'but it would bring harm to others, so it can't be right.'

'Then, you might want to revise your statement,' said Hypatia.

'Okay,' I started, 'right is what is beneficial to oneself and not harmful to others and it should be determined in this manner.'

'What about suicide, is it right or wrong?' asked Hypatia.

'It is wrong,' I answered.

'But the person committing suicide would be doing something he thinks beneficial to himself and won't be harming others in the process,' said Hypatia. 'Why is it wrong?'

'But harm doesn't have to be physical to be considered as harm,' I said. 'In this case, the person would have harmed the people close to him on an emotional level.'

'Let us then take the example of a person who has no family or friends and who has lots of problems in life,' said Hypatia. 'Wouldn't suicide be beneficial to him as a form of mercy and, at the same time, he wouldn't be harming any other person?'

'It would be as you said, but nothing justifies suicide. It is wrong,' I said.

'So this rule can't be used to determine what's right and wrong?' said Hypatia.

'No, it can't. We are back to square one,' I said.

'Don't be negative,' spoke Hypatia. 'We've learned so much through our examinations so far. Therefore, don't stop now; give me your next rule so that we may examine it.'

'Actually, I don't have any,' I replied.

'It's fine. Maybe it is time for me to give you a hand in this,' said Hypatia.

'That would be great,' I said.

'Let's take, for example, a gardener with three plants,' started Hypatia. 'The gardener didn't water the first plant at all, he watered the second plant moderately, and he watered the third plant excessively. What's going to happen to each of the three plants?'

I replied, 'The first one is going to die because it wasn't given any water. The second one is going to grow up fine. The third one is going to drown because it was given too much water.'

'That is correct,' said Hypatia. 'And so, what is the right thing to do when it comes to watering plants.?'

'The right thing will be,' I said, 'to give plants a moderate amount of water. Giving them no water or too much water is the wrong thing.'

'How did you come to that conclusion?' asked Hypatia.

'By what happened to the plants,' I said. 'I see it now! It was the outcomes that showed me what is right and what is wrong. Could it be that outcome is the determinant that we have been looking for?'

'I don't know, let's examine it,' said Hypatia.

'Let's do it!' I said enthusiastically. 'Every action has an outcome and depending on the outcome, right and wrong are determined.'

'So you're saying that if the outcome is good then the action is right and vice versa?' asked Hypatia.

'Yes,' I answered.

'Therefore, the outcome holds more importance than the action, right?' said Hypatia.

'Supposedly,' I replied.

'Tell me,' spoke Hypatia, 'do you consider stealing money in order to give to the poor right or wrong?'

'Of course, it is wrong,' I said.

'But the outcome, which is giving to the poor, is good, isn't it?' asked Hypatia.

'Yes, it is good,' I answered.

'If the outcome is good, why is it that the action is wrong then?' said Hypatia.

'Because the means to it is evil,' I replied.

'Correct,' said Hypatia. 'A basic principle in morality is that we cannot do evil in order to achieve good. Otherwise, we could justify doing just about any evil in the world.'

'You're right,' I replied.

'Outcomes are not a reliable way, or a determinant, to judge whether an action is right or wrong. Lots of "good" outcomes could be attained through bad means.' Hypatia continued, 'Let's take this example, if you steal some money, what is the action here?'

'Stealing,' I replied.

'Correct, and what is the outcome?' said Hypatia.

'Me gaining more money?' I said, unsurely.

'Also correct,' said Hypatia. 'Now, what will happen after you have stolen the money?'

'Well, if I get caught, I will go to jail and people around me will resent me,' I said. 'But if I don't get caught, nothing is going to happen.'

'Very good,' said Hypatia, 'and this stage after the outcome, it is the consequences of the action, isn't it?'

'Right,' I replied.

'Would you say the consequences you mentioned were good or bad?' asked Hypatia.

'Bad,' I answered.

'So, even though the outcome of stealing is good for you,' said Hypatia, 'it brought bad consequences, correct?'

'Correct,' I replied.

'And every action will surely have some consequences to it, right?' said Hypatia.

'For sure,' I replied.

'Can we say then that right and wrong are known and determined through consequences?' suggested Hypatia.

'Before I answer you that, there is something I need to address,' I said. 'In the previous example, we had another consequence of stealing and not getting caught—would this be an indicator of a good consequence?'

'That's a good question,' said Hypatia. 'Tell me, Nate, is good or doing good something to be ashamed of?'

'Of course, not. It would be honorable,' I said.

'What about doing something bad, will it bring shame?' said Hypatia.

'Yes, it will,' I replied.

'And when doing something shameful, will one talk about it publicly or keep it obscure and secret from the public?' said Hypatia.

'Of course, one will try to keep it secret,' I replied.

'In our example of stealing,' said Hypatia, 'if the person doesn't get caught, would he speak about his act publicly or would he keep it a secret?'

'He'll keep it a secret for sure, for it will bring shame to him and it can get him arrested as well,' I said.

'Knowing all that, would you say that the second consequence is good or bad?' said Hypatia.

'It will be bad,' I said. 'Now, I understand.'

'Then, can we use consequences to determine what's right and what's wrong?' asked Hypatia.

'I think we can, I don't see anything false in this way,' I answered.

'In conclusion,' spoke Hypatia, 'there are many circumstances one might find himself in, along with even more actions bringing about limitless outcomes leading to countless consequences. And it is through the consequences of an action in a particular circumstance that it is determined if that action is right or wrong.'

'Well said, Hypatia,' spoke Plato. 'And very good, Nate. You two put forward an interesting conversation that I'm glad to have witnessed.'

Plato's words made me more confident, and conversing with Hypatia, little by little, drove away the fear I had at the beginning of the conversation and the doubt that I could hold such a conversation.

'Since you and Nate have finished, allow me to indulge in a little talk with you, Hypatia,' spoke Luqman.

'Sure, but let me visit the ladies' room real quick first.' Hypatia left the table.

Luqman turned to me. 'So, Nate, where are you from? You don't strike me as a person from Paris.'

'That's because I'm not. I'm originally from Houston, Texas, USA,' I answered.

'So you are an American?' said Luqman.

'Yes,' I replied.

'You're a far way from home, kid. What brings you all the way here?' said Luqman.

'My father works here and so he brought us all along with him. Right now, I'm attending school here,' I said.

'That's great! How long have you been living here?' said Luqman.

'More than one year now,' I replied with comfort. It was kind of lovely having to speak about common things after having the intense conversation with Hypatia.

'How do you like the city so far?' asked Luqman.

'Paris is very beautiful. I don't see how someone can't fall in love with it,' I answered. 'What I love about it is its atmosphere. I like the architectural style of its buildings, its nice weather, and its many beautiful places and cafes that you can just enjoy, alone or with your friends.'

Hypatia came back and said as she sat down on the sofa, 'I heard something about a beautiful place; where is it?'

Plato smiled and said, 'Nate was just saying that he loved the many cafes in Paris and their cosy atmosphere.'

'That makes two!' Hypatia raised her hand for a high-five. I wasn't sure of this quick relationship development and so I slowly high-fived Hypatia. Hypatia had the kind of personality that breaks the ice very quickly. As the rest of the group were keeping their cool and acting their ages, Hypatia didn't mind joking around once in a while and I liked that about her.

'Anyway, what is it that you wanted to talk to me about, Luqman?' asked Hypatia.

'Here we go,' spoke Luqman, taking a comfortable sitting position. 'The question or statement that you and Nate examined was "if there were no prophets or messengers sent and if there were no holy books, how are right and wrong determined?", wasn't it?'

'Yes, it was,' Hypatia replied.

'I see some crucial premises in your argument,' said Luqman. 'In your argument, you took the assumption of no prophets and holy books and applied it right in the moment of your conversation, thus removing them from history but keeping the effects of their teachings present. If you really want to examine your question, you need to start from the beginning, from the first society and the first civilization and see how right and wrong would be determined without divine guidance or foundation.

'So now, my question to you is, how would the first people of the first society of all humanity determine what's right and what's wrong?'

'That is a good point, Luqman,' said Hypatia. 'It is true that in my conversation with Nate, our assumption might have had the effects of the prophets' legacy, but I still see what we arrived at can be applied to your premise, which is right and wrong can be determined through the consequences of the actions. In which good consequences determine what's right and bad consequences determine what's wrong.'

'Let's take the example of the gardener with the three plants you used earlier with Nate, in which two plants died and one lived,' spoke Luqman. 'How did the gardener determine that the death of the plants was bad and the life of it was good to pursue? Or, in your example of stealing, how were the consequences of stealing determined to be bad?

'Don't forget that in our premise we're dealing with the first society and the first humans to ever live who, supposedly, were left to explore and discover the world around them as well as discover the meaning of human affairs, interactions, and social life. No moral guidelines or principles were given to them nor had they any laws or code of conduct. They were supposed to figure out and establish all of that. They didn't have any fundamentals in which to know virtue and vice, good and bad, and right and wrong. Taking what I just said into consideration, my question here would be, how are consequences determined as good or bad in the first place?'

'Good question, Luqman!' spoke Hypatia. 'How about trial and error? When we want to achieve something, we try and we try and every time we fail, we change the method we attempted and try a new method. We go on like this, learning from previous attempts until we achieve what we desire. Just like a doctor trying to find a cure to a disease. Every time he fails, he changes his approach until he finds the remedy.

'The same thing can be said about the example of the gardener and the three plants. The gardener tried three different watering approaches and, depending on the consequences, he knew which was good and which was bad.'

Luqman replied saying, 'Trial and error is a good approach, but the sole purpose of this approach is to find a way to achieve an already known and desired outcome or consequence, whether good or bad. But it cannot be used to determine whether an outcome or a consequence is good or bad.

'Allow me to elaborate: in the example you mentioned about the doctor, the doctor already knows the outcome he seeks, which is a remedy to cure the disease. And he knows that it is good. His only problem is he doesn't know how to achieve the desired outcome. That's why the method of trial and error works; since the outcome is known, there is something to judge and evaluate your trials by. Otherwise, the whole point of trial and error would be meaningless.

'As for the example of the gardener, when he sees the consequences, how would he determine which consequence is good and which is bad? Simply put, he can't. He can't make such a decision because he lacks the necessary knowledge to do so. Taking the circumstances of the gardener being one of the first humans to live on the earth, how could he know that the life of a plant is good and its death is bad? For all he knows, this could be the normal thing. How could he even know that watering is the needed action to begin with to try and do it?

'Therefore, since the method of trial and error depends on knowing the outcome or circumstances, it cannot be used to determine whether a circumstance is good or bad.'

'Very sound argument, Luqman, one that I can't oppose,' said Hypatia. 'How about primitiveness? I mean the same kind of nature or instinct that is found in animals. We see around us, in the animal kingdom, mothers taking care of their children, they protect them, some breastfeed their young while others, like birds, provide food for their young. There are also animals like cats digging a hole in the ground to defecate in and then cover. There are some animals like crows who dig a hole in the ground to bury their dead. There are also countless animals that build sophisticated buildings and structures which show intelligent design.

'Now tell me, what led those animals to build such a structure in their particular design? Or who taught mothers the care of their younglings? No one. Animals tend to get those behaviors within the years as they grow older by nature. This is what we call primitiveness.'

'I would agree that primitiveness leads animals to do what is good, at least for them, thus it can be used to determine what is good or bad,' Luqman continued. 'But we need to see if humans have some kind of primitiveness, just like animals. One major characteristic of primitiveness is that it is found among all members of a species and that it is earned by nature or instinct. But if a trait or a behavior was found among certain members and not others, then this is a characteristic of something that is learned and taught not earned by nature.

'When it comes to humans, some form of primitiveness can be seen in infants and babies, such as the seeking of their mothers' breasts whenever they are hungry; but as the child starts to grow older, he is shaped by the things taught to him and he slowly starts to lose his primitiveness. He will start to make and form his own beliefs, views, and values that may be unique to himself. When it comes to determining what is good and bad, I'm certain such matters shouldn't be decided by infants and babies but by grown-ups, even if they have no primitiveness left in them.'

'Actually, you have a point there,' spoke Hypatia. 'The nature found in animals, which we can call primitiveness, is not the same as the one found in humans. Humans differ from one another when it comes to nature, which makes it a subjective matter, thus it cannot be used as a determinant.'

'You are right,' said Luqman.

'I'm trying to find a determinant, but nothing comes to my mind right now,' said Hypatia.

'Let us start from the beginning,' spoke Luqman. 'We first sat out to find how to determine right from wrong and we arrived to the conclusion that consequences are used as the determinant, being that good consequences lead to what's right and bad ones lead to that which is wrong. We then set a goal to see how consequences themselves are determined as good or bad.

'In the example of the doctor and the cure, the doctor has some form of knowledge of what the outcome or consequence should be—the ability to cure the disease. And in the example of the gardener and the three plants, the gardener also has a knowledge of what the good outcome or consequence should be, which is life and fruition of the plant.

'Both examples share a common factor which is the knowledge of good and bad and this raises a serious question in our assumption of the first humans in the first society. That question is, how would those first people acquire such knowledge in the first place? The only way that I see fitting is through revelation. There has to be a person at the start of society, civilization, and humanity that was in connection with the divine, or God, and this person received the knowledge of what is good and what is bad. And through him, he relied this knowledge to the rest of humanity.'

'Well, revelation is a possible choice,' said Hypatia, 'and teaching people the knowledge of good and evil or good and bad is a fitting reason for why the messengers were sent; nonetheless, I still think there is a way of knowing what's right and what's right without divine intervention but don't know it yet.'

'That's fine,' said Luqman. 'Take your time with it, but please tell me when you have found a way.'

'Believe me, I will!' said Hyaptia with a smile.

'Well, that was amazing and insightful!' spoke Plato. 'Thank you all, Nate, Hypatia, and Luqman, for a wonderful conversation. I really learned a lot today.'

It was my first time holding a conversation with someone other than Plato. I was hesitant at the beginning and I doubted my reasoning and argumentation skills but Plato's compliment and his interest in my speech assured me and made me feel that becoming a philosopher was something that I could achieve one day. I felt quite happy about that.

'Well, I think I'm gonna call it a day,' said Luqman.

'Me too,' added Hypatia.

'You go ahead both of you,' said Plato. 'As for Nate and me, we will stay here for a bit longer. I have something to say to him.'

The feeling of happiness that I felt faded away as all I was thinking about was that I must have messed up in my arguments and now Plato wanted to have a one-to-one with me. I knew I wasn't perfect and that I was new to the art of conversations and that I should be happy with this assumption, but still, I was worried that I failed somewhere at the discussion and I couldn't stand the idea of failure.

'Okay, we'll leave you to it,' said Hypatia, giving me a good-luck thumbs-up.

CHAPTER 5

School of Pythagoras

Luqman and Hypatia had just left, leaving me and Plato sitting alone at the table. As I waited for Plato to finish drinking his tea, I started looking at and listening to a woman who was playing a grand piano that was in the café. She was playing Beethoven's "Moonlight Sonata" and she was good at it.

'Nate, you with me?' said Plato.

'Yeah, what is it that you wanted to talk to me about, Plato?' I asked.

'Don't worry, it's not a major topic,' answered Plato. 'I only have some information and advice to share with you.'

'Go ahead,' I replied.

'Did you notice how Luqman and Hypatia converse with each other?' said Plato.

'What do you mean?' I said.

'Even though they had different beliefs, they worked together in pursuit of the truth and that is exactly what a philosopher should do,' spoke Plato. 'You see, it is difficult to know for sure that you have the correct knowledge of something. You always need to account for the probability of your fault, even if it is a topic you are an expert in. If you don't do this, you close the doors of knowledge and wisdom and you'll forever be in ignorance.

'Knowing this and while conversing with others, if you approach conversations with the mentality of who's going to win and who's going to lose or who's going to humiliate whom, your ego will prevent you from learning anything and you might miss the very truth you're seeking. In such cases, your ego will tell you that if you accept the truth, you will be admitting defeat and so you will reject it.

'You need to approach conversations with an open mind and a desire to learn. You need to work together with the one you are conversing with. Be just and unbiased. Admit the falseness in your own logic and opinion, if there is any, and if your adversary lacks evidence for his logical point and you have it, give it to him. You need to see the situation as you and your adversary both working together and combining your minds to find a universal truth.'

'True,' I said.

'Let me tell you something about the Pythagorean school,' Plato continued. 'Students in the school of Pythagoras were split into three circles. Students of the first circle, the outer circle, were named the "Akousmatikoi" or the "Listeners". Those students were permitted to attend lectures that contains knowledge that was, in a way, common with the general public. Those students were under oath to never speak both in the lectures and outside to the public about the knowledge being studied. This phase or circle stretched for three years. Ones who graduate from it, go on to the next circle.'

'May I ask one question here?' I said.

'Go ahead,' replied Plato.

'Regarding the inner circle,' I said, 'if the knowledge taught there is common to the general public, why is it that students were banned from speaking about it?'

'Good question,' spoke Plato. 'The purpose here of silence is not to protect the knowledge from others but to protect students from themselves. You see, one of the great vices is the "Love of Speech" and I don't mean by that knowledge, wisdom, and conversation, but the love of fame that accompanies the ability of rhetoric and public speaking. The love to be known by the masses and to be glorified by them.'

'I get it now,' I said.

Plato continued, 'After graduation, one moves to the next circle, the inner circle, and joins the "Mathematikoi" or the "Learners". Those students are permitted to attend lectures that students of the previous circle are banned from. Lectures that are considered a bit secretive of the knowledge shared there. And just like the previous circle, they are under an oath of silence and they must study for five years before graduating and moving on to the next circle.

'In the next and last innermost circle, a student has truly been initiated into the Pythagorean Mystery School and is invited to the most secretive lectures and esoteric knowledge.'

'That sounds like a great system,' I said, 'but there is something I still don't get: why can't the students speak inside the lectures? What if they wanted to ask something or get an explanation?'

'I think you misunderstood,' said Plato. 'Students weren't allowed to speak in the lectures; they were only supposed to listen and reflect. As for the things you mentioned, any student can connect with the spokespersons outside the lectures and ask them whatever they want.'

'That sounds reasonable,' I said. 'But I don't understand why they can't speak in the lectures.'

'So they can endure the test of silence,' Plato replied.

'What do you mean?' I asked, really intrigued to know the answer.

'Students are put under eight years of silence before being initiated, so that they are tested in the trial of silence,' answered Plato. 'It might sound simple to keep your silence, but it is not an easy task, especially if one sees himself holding great news or knowledge that would glorify him in the eyes of the public.

'Don't underestimate this. Some people, when they learn something new, begin to talk about it in front of other people. And after they do such, they don't learn something new; instead, they find new people to tell the same information to, over and over. And if you meet such a person and see him again after many years, you would find that he is the same as you met him the first time, with no change.

'As for staying silent in the lectures, it is to combat the urge found in the ego to cut other people's speech in the middle to say one's own opinion. It is not enough to let others finish speaking before replying to them, you must first understand what they said before doing so. Not doing this will prevent one from gaining the wisdom other people might have, thus hindering him from gaining more knowledge. This is such a dangerous trait that, if not treated, could leave one assuming he is knowledgeable while in fact he is ignorant.

'For these reasons, this oath was required, to beat the ego from drowning in the love of speech. Students are tested against silence for eight years and any student who cannot keep his silence, is condemned not worthy to be initiated into the esoteric knowledge that the Pythagorean Mystery School offered. For such knowledge must be kept secret from the public and the uninitiated.

'And the reason I'm telling you all of this is that you need to follow the same philosophy. You are at a young age and your heart is empty like an empty land that will take anything thrown in it. You might learn something new to you and think it is the truth, but trust me, later among the years, you'll find a new perspective that will render the old one false. You are at the age where you need to learn and take before you can start giving. Give yourself time and don't be hasty to show the knowledge you've gained, for maybe what you have learned and think is true is false after all. I know there is comfort in speaking out what is inside of your chest, but you need to resist it, especially if you didn't find people for that kind of speech.

'Do you understand what I have just told you, Nate?'

'Yes, I do. It makes sense, actually,' I replied. Plato answered a question that I'd been struggling with for weeks. It is through years of experience and learning that one could be really wise. Wisdom doesn't come within a night, it requires patience, determination, and above all a good heart. Now, I realized my stage in this journey, if I can call it a stage. I was at the stage of silence and learning. I shouldn't be eager to talk to people to show my wisdom, or lack of it, which—since I know myself—would surely anger me and bring me down. Instead, I should strive after Wisdom the right way, through patience and determination in learning about the world around.

'I'm glad it did,' said Plato. 'Now, excuse an old man like me, for I grow tired and need to head back to my home and rest.'

'No problem, I also need to go back,' I said. 'Thank you very much for this small talk. I really learned a lot and I really enjoyed it.'

'My pleasure!' replied Plato with a smile.

With this, Plato and I left the café and went on our separate ways. On my way home, I reflected on Plato's words in silence. It was amazing how an inaction could have so many meaningful actions to it. And I also remembered an old proverb, which made more sense now" "If speech was of silver, then silence is of gold".

CHAPTER 6

Perfection

Plato had texted me informing me of a gathering he and his friends were having one evening at the café. I came at the time he specified and at the café entrance, I came across Hypatia.

'Hello, Nate! How are you?' Hypatia said to me.

'I'm fine. How about you?' I replied to her.

'Pretty good,' she said. 'I didn't expect to see you tonight.'

'Yeah, Plato texted me and asked me to come,' I replied.

'I'm glad he did. A person your age should seek the company of grown-ups,' Hypatia said. 'I think you will really benefit from the conversations occurring in our group.'

'I really do benefit from them and I find them very interesting,' I said. 'I even noticed some change in me because of them.'

'What kind of change?' asked Hypatia.

'Before I started hanging out with you,' I spoke, 'I used to watch movies and TV series for the action scenes in them; I never cared about the story. Now, I would choose a good story over mindless action. I even see myself looking for well-written dialogue between characters. I know this might seem silly.'

'Silly, no. I think that is amazing! That is exactly what I look for in movies and TV series as well,' said Hypatia. 'Come, we shouldn't be standing outside.'

Afterward, Hypatia and I entered the café and saw that Plato and Protagoras were already there sitting together at a table. We went to them and joined their table.

'Good evening, everyone,' I greeted.

'Good evening, Nate!' replied Protagoras.

'Good evening, Nate!' said Plato. 'I'm glad you were able to come.'

'Of course. I wouldn't miss it for the world,' I replied.

'Hello, everyone! What are we discussing tonight?' said Hypatia.

Plato laughed and said, 'This is typical Hypatia, straight to business!'

Hypatia started speaking with a silly tone saying, 'Of course, why do you think I hang out with you folks? To have normal chit chat, hell no! Leave that stuff for Claire and her girlfriends and leave the serious discussions for Hypatia—'

'And her girlfriends!' interrupted Plato, and the group started laughing, me included.

I was so surprised to hear someone's true name at this group. I don't know why, but real names seemed like a secret thing in this group. Plato was the closest person to me among the group and I didn't even know his real name. Hypatia's real name suited her. With her long, blonde hair and white skin, she looked like a Claire.

'Nah! You're too old for that!' said Hypatia, teasing Plato.

'Ouch!' said Protagoras.

'I was referring to you as well,' said Hypatia.

'What! I'm only 35 years old. I ain't no old hag!' replied Protagoras.

'What's that supposed to mean?!' replied Plato.

Hypatia chuckled for a moment and said, 'Enough of that, let's get to business. What's the topic for tonight?'

I really like Hypatia. She had a charming charisma and a way of bringing delight to the group through her joyful and lively little acts.

'Tonight's topic is Perfection,' said Plato.

Another beautiful coincidence that I'd noticed was that whenever the group gathered to discuss a big topic, like Knowledge before, the perfect atmosphere followed as well. Like tonight, the café wasn't overcrowded, it had enough people in it to drive away the feeling of being in a ghost town and to create a bubbling background of voices that weren't annoyingly loud but blended seemingly with the place. Also, the yellow light of the chandeliers and the candlesticks was reflecting heavenly off the gilded interior decoration that really showed the Rococo royal design at its best. And to top it all, the pianist that night was playing soft melodies that added to the atmosphere and didn't fight for the listener's attention.

Plato started speaking, 'Perfection... this is a topic that has intrigued me the past couple of days and I want to put an end to it. That is the reason why I have set up this gathering, for I would like us tonight to discuss what Perfection is and what does it mean? But before we start, I would like to get something out of the way first.

'I know Perfection can be many different things to equally different people, and that people say that you cannot state definitely if something is perfect or not because the judging criteria differ from one person to another. This kind of view puts perfection on the subjectivity side; whether that's true or not, I don't want us to have a discussion regarding subjectivity. The very significance of that word means there is no right or wrong, and discussing a topic subjectively is a waste of time, at least for me, for there is no definitive correct answer to it.

'That being said, let's try defining what perfection is objectively, or rather, see if there is an objective definition to it. Let's open this discussion with the following question, when can we say that something is perfect?'

'First of all, let me say that I agree with you on your stand on subjectivity and I am more eager than you to examine perfection on the scale of objectivity,' spoke Hypatia. 'Could it be that something is perfect when it is without flaws or deficiency?'

'That is an interesting statement worthy of examination,' said Plato. 'Let's start with, what do you mean by flaws?'

'A flaw is anything that is considered as a fault or a deformity,' said Hypatia.

'What about deficiency?' said Plato. 'How would you define it?'

Hypatia replied with, 'Deficiency is the lacking or shortcoming of something.'

'What's the difference between flaw and deficiency?' asked Plato.

'Flaw is a fault resulted from a thing that exists in the object itself while deficiency is a fault resulted from a thing being missing from the object,' answered Hypatia.

'Very good. Why would flaw and deficiency prevent something from being or reaching perfection?' asked Plato.

'Because, by nature, they are something that is disliked and undesirable,' answered Hypatia. 'A thing that has a feature that is considered as faulty, whether because it is broken or bad by itself, has a flaw. And a thing that has a necessary feature missing from it, is considered to have a deficiency.'

'Therefore, you said that perfection is something without a flaw and deficiency, right?' said Plato.

'That is correct,' replied Hypatia.

'A thing without flaws or deficiencies is surely a good thing but how would you know that it is perfect?' said Plato.

'What do you mean?' replied Hypatia.

'Allow me to rephrase my question,' said Plato. 'How do you recognize a flaw? How do you know that something has a flaw or a thing is a flaw to begin with?'

'The only way I see is by knowing a better version of the thing itself,' said Hypatia. 'This way, by comparing similar things, or objects, you will be able to recognize the flaws in the inferior object. For example, take two similar cars, one with perfect tires, and the other with one puncture tire. For sure the punctured tire is a flaw in the car.'

'And deficiency will go on in the same manner, wouldn't it?' asked Plato.

'Yes, it would. Continuing with the two-cars example, if one of the cars has a missing tire, it would be an example of a deficient feature,' answered Hypatia. 'You see, by comparing two things, we will be able to recognize the missing features that would make a thing better.'

'We're here speaking about features and traits, aren't we?' said Plato.

'Yeah,' replied Hypatia.

'Those features ought to be perfect in order to be worthy of being compared to, right?' asked Plato.

'Necessarily,' replied Hypatia.

'And if those perfect features are known,' spoke Plato, 'there is no need to examine and compare an object against another similar one; it can be directly compared against those perfect features, isn't that right?'

'Right,' replied Hypatia.

'This means your definition of perfection needs perfect references, isn't that right?' said Plato.

'Right again, Plato!' replied Hypatia, giving Plato a teasing look and a smile.

Plato smiled and continued, 'And so, a question must be asked here which is, how do you know that those references are perfect by themselves in the first place?'

Hypatia sighed and said, 'that is a good question. Perfect references must be set. And if we go on with the idea that their perfection is measured by the absence of flaws and deficiencies, then the question of how those flaws and deficiencies are recognized will be stated on and on with no end.'

'You are right about that,' said Plato.

'In this case, flaws and deficiencies won't cut it,' said Hypatia. 'We need to find another way to define Perfection.'

'That we must,' said Plato.

When Claire, or Hypatia, first suggested her definition, I thought that she had found the correct definition for Perfection. I never expected things to turn around this way.

'What about additions and subtractions?' spoke Protagoras. 'Somethings need other things to be added to them to be perfect. And on other occasions, they need other things to be taken, or subtracted from them, to be perfect. Thus, a thing is perfect when it doesn't need any addition to it or subtraction from it.'

'That is an interesting choice,' said Plato. 'I have to ask, how would additions and subtractions prevent perfection?'

Protagoras replied with, 'Perfection is perfect the way it is. Any addition made to perfection can mean either of two things. First, if it reaches perfection after the addition, then this means it wasn't perfect in the first place. Second, if it doesn't reach perfection after the addition, then this means it is imperfect right now, for any addition to perfection will always equal imperfection. And the same manner of examination goes for subtraction, leaving only that Perfection is something that doesn't need any addition or subtraction.'

'Well said, Protagoras,' said Plato. 'Now, what kinds of additions or subtractions can be applied?'

'To put it simply, there can be good ones and bad ones,' replied Protagoras.

'How are the good ones and the bad ones identified as such?' asked Plato.

'The additions or subtractions that lead to perfection are good while those leading to, and resulting in, imperfection are bad,' answered Protagoras.

'In that case,' spoke Plato, 'we ought to ask ourselves, how do we know that the additions and subtractions have led to perfection or imperfection?'

Protagoras thought for a moment and said, 'I think we've reached the same dead end as with Hypatia's theory. Without a perfect reference, it will be hard to judge additions and subtractions.'

'Both your and Hypatia's theories can surely be considered as features of Perfection, but they are not necessarily a way to identify it.' Plato continued. 'But there is something that intrigued me about your theory, Protagoras.'

'What is it?' asked Protagoras.

'Let's examine the following example,' started Plato. 'Let's imagine we have a car and we removed two tires from it—is that a good subtraction or a bad one?'

'It is for sure a bad one,' replied Protagoras.

Plato continued saying, 'Let's add those two tires that we have removed earlier to the car— is that a good addition or a bad one?'

'A good one,' replied Protagoras.

'Very good,' Plato continued. 'Now, let's add a helicopter rotor to the car, is that a good addition or a bad one?'

I didn't understand what a helicopter rotor was. Hypatia noticed my confused face and said to me in a low voice while whirling her index finger, 'It's the helicopter fan.'

I didn't say anything back to Hypatia, instead, I smiled and nodded to her. I felt a little embarrassed that she noticed me.

'I would say it is a bad addition,' Protagoras said in reply to Plato's question. 'I don't see any benefit in adding a helicopter rotor to a car.'

'Tell me, Protagoras,' spoke Plato, 'why did you choose your answers the way you did? What did you base your answers on?'

'Well, I thought of the car and its ability to work well,' said Protagoras. 'Without wheels, the car won't be able to move and so removing the tires is a bad subtraction, while adding the tires is a good addition.'

'Very good,' said Plato. 'And what about the addition of the helicopter rotor—why is it a bad addition? For sure, an airborne car is a great thing.'

'Not necessarily,' said Protagoras. 'The idea of an airborne car might be good, but its functionality might prove otherwise. Think about it this way: will a car with a rotor move effectively on the ground without any setbacks and will it be effectively mobile in the air?'

'Spot on thinking, Protagoras! You exactly touched the point I was making,' said Plato. 'In your justifications, weren't you speaking about the functionality of the car?'

'Yes, I was,' replied Protagoras.

'Didn't you judge the goodness or badness of the additions and subtractions based on functionality as well?' said Plato.

'Yes, I did,' replied Protagoras.

'We agreed earlier that good additions and subtractions lead to perfection,' Plato continued. 'Also, since additions and subtractions are good as long as they adhere to the functionality of an object, functionality is associated directly with perfection.'

'I think we shouldn't be jumping to conclusions so quickly; we should give it more thought,' said Protagoras.

'Let us then judge Hypatia's theory of flaws and deficiencies on the basis of functionality,' spoke Plato. 'Continuing with the car example, if a car has a flat tire, is this a case of a flaw or a deficiency?'

'It would be a case of a flaw since we agreed that a flaw is a fault existing in the object itself,' said Protagoras.

'What about the case of a missing engine—is it a flaw or a deficiency?' asked Plato.

'It would be a deficiency case since the fault is missing from the object itself,' answered Protagoras.

'Correct answers,' said Plato. 'Now, will the two cases of flaw and deficiency affect the functionality of the car or not?'

'Of course, they will. The car won't be able to function properly with either of them,' replied Plato.

'Since all flaws, deficiencies, good and bad additions and subtractions affect the perfection of objects through their functions,' said Plato, 'then function is the main determinant of perfection; would you agree to that?'

Protagoras didn't reply and stayed silent, lost in his thoughts. Plato saw Protagoras' deep thinking and said, 'Let me elaborate more on my stance on function. Since the functionality of an object is necessary for its perfection, it is crucial that things function in accordance with the reason they were made in the first place.

'Take for example a fruit knife. Such a knife will be considered as perfect as long as it is able to function as it is intended to. The moment it becomes unable to cut fruits it will become imperfect following the same logic. And if such a knife was tested on a piece of meat, surely it won't be able to cut it, but that will not affect its perfection, as cutting meat wasn't one of the reasons a fruit knife was made for.'

'So, following your logic,' spoke Protagoras, 'things will be judged on perfection based on the reason they were made. Since things vary on their qualities, everything should have its own scale of judgement, or standards, as different things made for different reasons can't be judged on the perfection scale of other greater or lesser things, isn't that right, Plato?'

'Exactly,' replied Plato.

'Would you mind, Plato, defining what Perfection is? It will help make things much clearer,' requested Hypatia.

To be honest, Plato's example of the car earlier got me confused and I'd been a little lost ever since. I really wanted a direct answer to get me back on track, but the fact that Hypatia asked Plato to share a direct definition got me wondering if she had noticed my lost thoughts and only asked Plato in order to help me.

'Of course,' said Plato. 'Perfection is the ability of things to function as they are supposed to.'

'It seems like a good definition so far,' spoke Protagoras. 'But I have a couple of concerns about function that need to be addressed.'

'Sure, tell me what's on your mind,' replied Plato. 'Isn't that what we are here for?'

This discussion had been a rollercoaster of highs and lows. Every time someone suggested a definition of what Perfection was, it was examined and then proven wrong. I found it very exciting and attention-grabbing.

'If we're speaking about the function of a thing as its perfection,' spoke Protagoras, 'we need to speak about an important aspect regarding function, which is development.'

'What do you mean?' replied Plato.

'I'm speaking about enhancing the way a thing performs its function.' Protagoras continued, 'Sometimes, there is more than one way for a thing to perform its function. Let us examine an example to make this point clearer, but before we do, please answer this question: what is the function of trains?'

'To put it in the simplest form,' Plato started answering, 'the main purpose of trains is to be able to move on rails and get from one location to another.'

Protagoras continued with, 'Excellent! Now, let's take a coal train and an electrical train as an example. Both of the trains are able to achieve the purpose that you mentioned earlier, but one of them can do it in a more efficient way. So, which train of the two would you say is perfect?'

'I get your point and it is a very good one,' spoke Plato. 'Before I answer your question, let me first say that improvements can either be in the same field or in different ones. In your example, the first train runs on coal while the second one runs on electricity. This improvement happened in different fields to achieve the same purpose. An example of an improvement happening in the same field would be that of two electrical trains, the second one functioning much better than the first one, let's say in speed. In this example, there was an advancement in technology that facilitated the increase of speed of the second train.

'Considering the nature of development, there will always be a much better way of performing a function and there will always be an improvement. Every state-of-the-art thing will be perfect at its time and imperfect in the long run, for the future can hold countless and various enhancements. So, to answer your question, I'd say, at the time that electricity was the high-tech benchmark of the day in trains, not considering the electromagnetism of today, the electric train is the perfect one while the coal train is the imperfect one.'

'Very good, Plato, but tell me,' said Protagoras, 'why is it that performing the function is not enough to reach perfection? Why does it have to function in the best way and shape possible?'

'This has to do with one of Perfection's essential features which is being the best,' said Plato. 'Perfection has always been the mark of the highest standards in everything, a mark that is not easily obtained by anyone or anything. It is a crown that is worn only by a single thing in each particular field and no more than one can lay a claim to it.

'Think of the consequences that will follow if the standards of Perfection were ever lowered. In that case, its quality will drop and many will be able to achieve it and lay claim to its title. This in turn, will eliminate competition and the need to strive for progress and innovation which, without a doubt, will result in the eradication of development in general.'

'Well said, Plato, but there is one thing regarding function and development that I think needs to be addressed.' Protagoras continued. 'So far, we have spoken about development as a continuous process that will never end and will always see improvements along the passage of time. Whether absolute perfection can be achieved or not, we must not leave it aside without examination.'

'I agree with you. We must define the state of absolute Perfection,' said Plato, 'but just to be in the same page, absolute perfection is the same as perfection, we are only using the term "absolute" to clarify that we are speaking about the state of perfection where there is no further functional improvement that can be done to a thing.'

'Of course,' said Protagoras.

'Regarding function and perfection,' spoke Plato, 'the more optimal a function is, the more it gets closer to perfection. Since absolute perfection is the state where there is no further improvement or enhancement, it is only fair to say that absolute perfection is an ultimate state. And such a state is characterized by having limits, which are the points where there is no going beyond.

'Applying this to our example of the electrical train, when one of the train features, like speed, mobility, braking, or other performances reaches its ultimate state, then that feature has truly achieved Perfection. But since we are speaking about a hypothetical limit, one that we can't ever be sure if we have achieved or not, the state-of-the-art status will suffice as Perfection.'

'You've explained your stance of function and development quite well, Plato' said Protagoras. 'That being said, I think you need to rephrase your initial definition of Perfection, just so that we maintain a clear picture.'

'Sure thing,' said Plato. 'Perfection is the ability of things to function as they are supposed to, in the most optimal way.'

'I think that's an excellent definition,' said Protagoras.

'Thank you,' spoke Plato. 'Is there any doubt about this definition or any point we should investigate regarding Perfection? In the end, we mustn't rush such an important matter and we should examine every angle possible.'

'Nothing from my side,' replied Protagoras.

'As for me, I have a point that I think is worth checking out,' spoke Hypatia, 'which is the point of Beauty.'

'What do you mean by that?' asked Plato.

'Let me explain in an example.' Hypatia continued, 'imagine we have two cars that are identical, performance-wise, but differ in their interior decoration. The first car has seats made of vinyl and an interior made of suede while the other car has seats made of nylon and an interior made of wood and leather. Now, which car of the two would you say is perfect and which one is imperfect?'

Plato stayed silent for a while thinking and when he took too long, Hypatia cried, 'I've finally done it! I have finally made Plato speechless with no answer!'

Plato smiled and replied back, 'Honestly, I was only speechless because I was shocked that you knew so much about cars. I didn't know you to have interest in these kinds of things.'

Protagoras chuckled at Plato's response and I smiled.

Hypatia laughed and said, 'Don't change the subject; answer my question, Plato.'

'Speaking seriously now,' started Plato, 'it is hard right now to say which car is perfect and which one is imperfect in your example. It depends on the functional need of the materials in question. Some materials are more comfortable than others, some are more luxurious, some easier to clean, some last longer, and so on. In the end, it depends on the personal use and need.'

'So you're saying it is a subjective thing, right?' said Hypatia with an ingenious smile.

'You fox! You lured me into a trap,' replied Plato with a smile.

'Just admit it! Subjectivity is a thing here,' said Hypatia.

'Or maybe I was wrong in my argumentation,' defended Plato.

'No, no! I think you made a pretty solid one,' said Hypatia.

'Well... can you prove it?' requested Plato.

'Don't worry, I will.' As Hypatia said this, I swore I could jump off my seat out of excitement. I liked most in these conversations the back and forth of logic and reasoning; it never got old. 'Decorations, ornamentations, and other beauty-related things are all associated with taste. Taste is the likability and preferability towards aesthetic things from shapes and colors to sensations and feelings. People tend to have different and various tastes towards countless things. Tastes that are, many times, conflicting with one other. Consequently, taste is subjective in nature and there is no way to objectify it, at least in a specific matter. What I mean by my last sentence is, between a clean car and a dirty one, everyone will prefer the clean one for sure, as this is a general matter. But, if the two cars were clean and they only differ in the outer color, people will have different tastes and preferability to what they see as the perfect color for them. Now, this matter is a specific one and it can only be subjective. As a result, since Beauty is related to taste, and what people find tasteful is subjective, Beauty is therefore a subjective matter.'

'Well said, Hypatia. I agree with your argumentation,' said Plato. 'Since Beauty is a subjective matter and Perfection is an objective matter, also, since opposites can't be joined together, Beauty then isn't taken as a considerable aspect of Perfection, as how flaws and deficiencies are. Therefore, we are back to our latest definition of what Perfection is, which is the one associated with function at its optimal performance.'

'In that you are correct, Plato,' said Hypatia. 'But that doesn't change one fact.'

'Which fact are you speaking about?' asked Plato.

'The fact that you agreed to the existence of subjectivity!' answered Hypatia, in a teasing way.

Plato smiled and said, 'Yes, yes, I agreed! What's the big deal?'

'The deal is that you hardly ever get convinced by other people,' Hypatia continued speaking in the same teasing manner.

'That's not true, is it, Protagoras?' said Plato.

'Well… you can be like that sometimes,' replied Protagoras, playing along with Hypatia.

'Wait a second, the both of you.' Plato glanced at Alfred who was passing by and called out to him. 'Alfred, could you come here for a second?'

Alfred came to our table and said, 'How can I help you, Plato?'

'Just a simple question,' spoke Plato. 'These two say that I don't get convinced by other people's arguments so easily; is that true?'

Alfred noticed Hypatia winking at him behind Plato's back. He understood what was going on and decided to play along saying, 'Well, sir, you can be hard to convince sometimes.'

'And what if I told you that I was convinced by an argument just now?' said Plato.

'Then I would hypothetically drop the tray I'm holding, with everything on it, on the ground out of disbelief.' As Alfred finished speaking, Hypatia, along with Protagoras, burst into laughter. I too had a laugh in me, but I suppressed it so as not to appear rude to Plato.

'Not you also, Alfred!' said Plato.

'Don't worry, sir, we are only teasing you,' said Alfred. 'You are not like that at all.'

Plato then turned to Hypatia and said to her while giving her a look, 'So that's how it is?'

Hypatia stopped laughing and said as she wiped out her laughter tears, 'Ah! I really needed that!'

'Anyway, sir, you got me curious,' spoke Alfred. 'What were you talking about? What is tonight's topic?'

'We were discussing the topic of Perfection and trying to find a definition to it,' replied Plato.

'And have you arrived at an answer?' asked Alfred.

'Yes,' Plato started answering, 'we concluded that Perfection is the ability of things to function as they are supposed to in the most optimal way.'

'What do you think of that?' asked Hypatia.

Alfred answered without taking a minute to reflect on the definition saying, 'That's absurd.'

Alfred's response took everyone by surprise, me included.

'Why do you say that?' asked Plato curiously.

'Well, let me ask you this, am I perfect?' Alfred asked back.

Plato thought it over for a moment and replied saying, 'I have no answer.'

Plato's answer confused me and suddenly, I was totally lost as to what was happening.

'So, you've got it, I see,' said Alfred. 'If you answered, "yes, I am perfect", then you will be implying that I was only created to serve others. And if you answered with "no", then you'll be saying that I can't do my job properly. In both ways, you'd be rude to me.'

The group stayed silent due to Alfred's revelation and no one replied back to him.

Alfred broke this silence saying, 'What content were you speaking in when you came up with this definition?'

'We were talking about trains and cars,' replied Plato.

'All right, I get you now. In that case, your definition is perfectly fine,' said Alfred.

'How so? After you've titled it with absurdism earlier?' asked Plato.

'Because earlier I didn't know which plane you were talking about and examining Perfection in,' answered Alfred.

'What do you mean by plane?' asked Hypatia.

'I'm not sure if I got the naming correct,' spoke Alfred, 'but there should be different... categories, let's call them, in which to examine Perfection. The categories are as follows: things made by man, nature excluding plants, plants, animals, humans, angels, and finally, God. Each one of these categories should have its own standards of Perfection. You cannot possibly hold a human-manufactured thing against the perfection of natural things, or compare plants' perfection with that of animals, or compare humans with angels.

'Your definition of Perfection works only on things created by humans, but it can't be used in other categories. For each category you need to find its own form of perfection.'

Alfred's remark left the group speechless. I could see in their faces the signs of astonishment and in their eyes the shock of having missed such an important point. As for me, I was shocked to hear that argument from Alfred. I had never spoken with him before.

Alfred noticed their shock as well and said, 'C'mon guys! How could you miss such a point? You are smarter than this.' With that, Alfred took his leave.

'We've been served!' said Hypatia, breaking the silence at last after a while.

'The man's got a point,' said Protagoras. 'And a crucial one at that.'

'We still need to figure out what perfection means in the other categories,' said Plato.

'Not we, you, both of you, need to find out,' said Hypatia. 'I, on the other hand, have some early classes to teach tomorrow morning and it's getting late.'

'What time is it?' Plato looked at his wrist watch and said, 'Look at the time; when did it get so late?'

'I think the rest of the topic will have to be postponed to another time,' suggested Protagoras.

'I also think that,' said Plato.

'Well, good. See you all later, ciao!' said Hypatia, who then took her leave.

'See you later,' Protagoras said to Hypatia as she left.

After that, we all left the café one by one. On the way home, I couldn't stop thinking about tonight's topic. I saw myself as a perfectionist. I liked to be the best at anything that I did. And when I fail at something, I get upset and depressed. I hated failure, or rather how I felt about it, and what it brought to me. Therefore, I thought perfection was a bad thing. The group spoke about Perfection as a good thing that should be sought after, but I still had mixed feelings about it. Perhaps my kind of perfection lay in a totally different category as Alfred suggested. Or perhaps my reaction towards failure was the bad thing while perfection was a good thing after all.

Despite all of that, I really enjoyed the drama, or comedy, that occurred between the group. I found it very refreshing to see the group behaving like that. I knew this might be a rare occasion for them to have such a comedy and that it might never happen again, but I was glad that I had witnessed it.

CHAPTER 7

To Whom Wisdom Should Be Spoken To

The next time, I came to the café straight from my class. I was sitting alone at a table, drowned in my own thoughts.

'Hi there!' said a voice near me.

I turned around and saw Luqman standing. 'Hi,' I replied.

'What's wrong?' Luqman said. 'When you come here, you usually look around to see if any of us are here. This time you came and sat all by yourself. Is something troubling you?'

'It's nothing,' I said in a low tone.

'C'mon, tell me,' insisted Luqman.

I stayed silent for a moment and then started speaking, 'Before, Plato and Protagoras had a discussion about Justice and Equality. Today in my class, this topic was brought up by a guy, a classmate of mine, who believed that Equality is Justice. I saw it as an opportunity to follow the same thought process that Plato did with this guy, but it went terribly.'

'What happened?' asked Luqman.

'At first, I talked to him about having a conversation about the matter and he agreed,' I said. 'But later, nothing went as I was expecting. He was very stubborn during the conversation. He didn't listen to my logic and interrupted me a lot of times. And I am so pissed off right now because of it.'

Luqman smiled and said, 'I understand, but let me ask you this. Who would you say was at fault?'

'What do you mean? Of course, he was,' I replied.

'Why?' asked Luqman.

'I'm not judging him for not believing in what I believe in,' I began, thinking I tackled Luqman's trick in his question. 'But I would say he is wrong because he didn't give me the chance to rationalize my opinion and tried to forced his on me.'

'That is correct,' said Luqman. 'What about you?'

'What about me?' I replied.

'Are you at fault or not?' said Luqman.

I stayed silent for a moment thinking about what Luqman actually meant and wanted by his question. I considered my attitude towards the guy but I couldn't recall being rude to him in any way. I considered my speech, but again, I didn't even get the chance to speak my stance on the matter. And lastly, since I'd tried to follow Plato's logic word by word, there was no way I could be wrong.

And when I couldn't find an answer, I replied saying, 'I don't see myself at fault. I did, or tried to do, the exact thought process that Plato did with Protagoras.'

'And what if I told you that you had had your own share of fault?' said Luqman.

'Why do you say that?' I replied.

'Let me ask you this,' spoke Luqman, 'do you think you are able to win every argument? By win, I mean convince the other person.'

'Of course not,' I said.

'Why is that? What factors are contributing here?' asked Luqman.

'I think the factor that is contributing into convincing others is Knowledge,' I answered. 'You can't convince someone who is more knowledgeable than you in a particular field or topic.'

Luqman replied, 'in that case, if you converse with someone in a topic you are more knowledgeable in, you should be able to convince him, correct?'

'Yes,' I replied.

'So, correct me if I'm wrong about this,' spoke Luqman, 'between you and your classmate, concerning the topic of Equity and Justice, I would say that you were, or are, the more knowledgeable one, right?'

'I believe so, yes,' I said.

'What about your classmate?' said Luqman. 'Didn't he also believe that he was more knowledgeable than you?'

'As a matter of fact, he did,' I said, 'by the fact that he kept interrupting me every time I said something he didn't believe in.'

'So you see,' spoke Luqman, 'this is the matter with all discussions, arguments, and debates between two or multiple people each thinking they are more knowledgeable than the other.'

I replied saying, 'I see, now. Knowledge can't be the determinant factor; there must be another one.'

'This is not the point right now,' interrupted Luqman. 'Regarding any topic, there are two types of people, those who have some kind of knowledge about it and those who are ignorant or have the wrong knowledge about it. For the sake of simplicity, let's just call them, a knowledgeable person and an ignorant one, all right?

'All right,' I replied.

'Do you think you can convince a knowledgeable person?' asked Luqman.

'Yes, I think so,' I answered.

'And what about an ignorant person, do you think you can convince him?' said Luqman.

'After my experience today with my classmate, I'm going to have to say no,' I replied.

'Why is that?' said Luqman.

I thought for a second and then replied, 'I don't know.'

'A knowledgeable person,' spoke Luqman, 'has a certain amount of knowledge that he is able to recognize the truth and admit when he is wrong. Whilst an ignorant person has no knowledge and he thinks that he has, and because of this, it is impossible to convince him with anything.'

'But sometimes I can teach someone something he is ignorant of,' I replied.

'We're not here talking about teaching,' said Luqman, 'we are talking about convincing.'

'What's the difference?' I asked.

Luqman said, 'In teaching, the student is admitting his ignorance of the matter and is willing and wanting to be taught. In convincing, you are trying to teach someone who thinks he knows better than you and thinks he doesn't want to be convinced or taught.'

'I understand now,' I said.

'So, let me ask you this again, what was your fault, or share of it?' said Luqman.

I thought for a moment and said, 'I'm sorry, I still don't know,'

'Wisdom doesn't not seek those who do not seek it,' said Luqman. 'You cannot go around speaking with everyone you meet. For every speech there are people for it. A wise man understands this and recognizes the types of people around him. He speaks wisdom to the wise and stays silent with those who are not, otherwise he will be put in a position of ridicule. Do you recognize your mistake now?'

'Yes, I do,' I said.

'Also, a good way to know the types of people out there is to interact and converse with them,' said Luqman.

'But wouldn't that put me in a lot of failing situations?' I asked Luqman, eager to hear his answer.

'Of course, it will. How do you expect to learn about anything without experience?' answered Luqman.

'So, you're saying that failure is a good thing?' I said.

'No, I'm saying that wisdom is gained through experience,' said Luqman. 'Do you remember our speech about Wisdom the other night, where we said that Wisdom is knowing right from wrong and doing what's right at the right moment?'

'Yes, I do,' I replied.

'Since half of Wisdom is intellectual and the other half is about applying the intellect in real life,' spoke Luqman, 'it is necessary to have hands-on experience with various matters in various situations to get to know what's right and when and what's wrong and when. Not everything can be taught and learned by word of mouth and some things need to be experienced to be understood.'

'So, failure can lead one to Wisdom, is that right?' I asked.

'Reflect on the following proverb, "There is no wise man without experience",' said Luqman. 'Experience leads to Wisdom. Success and failure are essential parts of experience. It is absolutely fine to make mistakes and fail from time to time and you certainly should not be afraid from trying something out of the fear of failure. If you let that type fear get to you, you will never accomplish anything in life.'

From Luqman's answer, I felt that he noticed my obsession with failure along with my fear of failure.

Luqman continued, 'One thing that should be added here is that what's most important about success and failure is how you react to them and what you learn from them. If you just accept the outcomes without understanding why they happened and what they really mean, then you'll be wasting the experience as if you never had it in the first place. Therefore, reflect on your experiences. Know the reasons for the successful ones to enhance them and understand the causes of the failed ones to eliminate them.'

With this, our conversation came to an end. Even though I didn't find Plato in the café that day, I was really glad to have had this conversation with Luqman and really excited to have learned this information about wisdom. But what I was most happy about was that Luqman had relieved me from the fear I had for failure. It was such an infuriating issue to me that I was happy it was gone now and I couldn't care less whether Luqman had noticed it in me or not, considering that he addressed me directly with his reply. Now, with this behind me, I could move forward and focus on things that truly contributed to the value of the mind.

CHAPTER 8

Love

'Hey, Alfred, can I ask you a question real quick?' I said to Alfred, who was passing near the table I was sitting at in the café.

'Sure, Nate. You can ask me anything,' replied Alfred.

'It's been a few days now that I've come here and have been me sitting alone without seeing any of the group. I have been wondering about something,' I spoke. 'What's the reason behind the decision of coming to the café without agreeing with others to meet here beforehand and only hoping to run into other members by chance? Wouldn't it be easier if they all agreed, via any social phone app, on a date and a time of meeting? Especially since there are not that many members in the group, which makes it even harder to run into someone by chance.'

Alfred laughed and said, 'I understand why you would think something like that considering the fact you haven't met all of the group.'

'Really? Who else is there that I haven't met?' I asked, a little curious.

'I don't know. Tell me who have you met from the group?' replied Alfred.

I answered, 'I've met Plato, Hypatia, Luqman, Protagoras and… that's pretty much it.'

'You haven't even come close to half of the group,' said Alfred.

'Really! Who else is there that I haven't met yet?' I replied, really intrigued now.

'I could tell you their names, or rather nicknames, but it is better for you to get introduced to them by meeting them in person,' said Alfred.

'Where are they? I've been coming here for a few months and I haven't met any of them,' I said.

'To your luck, most of them are out of town, if I recall correctly.' Alfred continued, 'Nonetheless, when they're all in town, there won't be a day on the weekend where you'd come here to the café and not run into one of them.'

'I understand,' I said. 'Now, the decision of just coming here without any further notice seems reasonable.'

'You know what, kiddo,' spoke Alfred, 'since there isn't much work in the café right now, is it all right if I sat down with you and have a little conversation?'

'Of course,' I replied. Alfred's request interested me and I was eager to hear what he had to say.

After a while, Alfred came and joined my table, bringing with him his own tea.

'Sorry to keep you waiting,' said Alfred.

'It's ok,' I replied. 'So, what is it that you wanted to talk to me about?'

'These guys, I mean the members of the group, have had a lot of conversations over the years, some I've had the pleasure of listening to while some I didn't.' Alfred continued, 'One of those conversations that I was lucky to hear just came to my mind, which I think you're going to like, and I want to share it with you. If you have the time, of course?'

'Of course, I have the time and the interest to hear it,' I replied. I was really excited to hear what Alfred had to say. Alfred's short white hair and chevron-style mustache reminded me of my grandfather who I used to sit down with and listen to his many stories. I had loved that very much.

'Before we start,' spoke Alfred, 'let me mention the people who were in the conversation. The first two you already know, Plato and Luqman, while the other two you haven't met yet; they are named, or nicknamed, Laozi and Hermes.'

'Back in the day,' Alfred began, 'I was working as a bartender in a bar downtown. The bar was classic and had dim, blue lighting giving a wonderful, cosy atmosphere to the place. One night, where there weren't many costumers, four people entered the bar and, despite the many empty tables, they sat at a corner of the bar counter, two on each side. To this day, I remember the drinks that I served them. I served Scotch to Plato, gin martini to Hermes, whiskey to Laozi, and a Shirley Temple to Luqman. It was a day that I would never forget. After all, it was also the day that I met these guys.

'Anyway, after I served them their drinks, I stood nearby cleaning and polishing glasses where I was able to hear their conversation clearly, as it wasn't a busy night and there wasn't much hubbub in the bar.

'Plato came in and asked Hermes what he would like to talk about.' Alfred paused and looked at me. 'I remember that Hermes said it wasn't so much a discussion as a speech, and Laozi wanted to know what he meant. Well,' Alfred said, taking a sip of his tea, 'Hermes told us he had just read Plato's *The Symposium* and he wanted to hear our ideas on Love. Everybody praised the idea and Laozi went on to share his thoughts about Love saying,

"Everything in existence is in constant movement of vibration, from the corporeal to the incorporeal. Everything vibrates, nothing rests. Vibration has a large bandwidth of frequency and everything vibrates in a different frequency. Some things vibrate in high frequencies while others vibrate in low ones. Those who vibrate in high frequencies are incorporeal or spiritual in nature whilst those who vibrate in low frequencies are corporeal or material in nature. An example of things of lower frequency would be anything that is tangible like earthly and watery bodies. Whilst an example of things of higher frequency would be anything perceptible by feelings like air, fire, and light.

"Light is the element that resonates the highest among the elements, and so, it's of the highest purity. Light has a large bandwidth of frequencies. There are many different lights, or radiations, that vibrates at different frequencies, the highest among them is known as the Empyrean light. Souls are spiritual bodies made of light. They are of the highest resonating incorporeal bodies but being trapped in corporeal ones makes their resonance receptible to change.

"Let us now focus our attention to the human soul. The soul and the body are interconnected together via the chakra system, an energy system. Actions influence the chakras, and the chakras influence the resonance of the soul. Good actions will feed the chakras with positive energy, thus increasing their vibrations, and the chakras in turn will make the soul resonate in a higher frequency. Bad actions will feed the chakras with negative energy, thus decreasing their vibrations, and the chakras, in turn, will make the soul resonate in a lower frequency. The higher the frequency of a soul is, the purer and light-like it is, and the lower the frequency of a soul is, the more impure and dark-like it is. We can summarize the relation between the body and soul in the mentioned regard with the following sentence; the body is the tuning tool of the soul.

"The bandwidth of souls is wide and vast. Similar frequencies attract and are attracted to each other while different frequencies repel from each other. The closer the frequencies of souls are to each other, the more harmonious they are with each other, whether they are resonating in low or high frequencies. The feeling that is produced by harmony is what we call Love.

"Love is not exclusive and limited to one person only; instead, it is felt with the souls that are resonating in frequencies closer to each other. Love can be felt with any human no matter what the relation is, whether it is parental, fraternal, filial, spousal, or that of relatives and friends. Also, love can be felt with all sorts of animals as they have souls themselves.

"Harmony produces two kinds of feelings; one that is produced in higher frequencies which is Love and one that is produced in lower frequencies which is Lust. Love should never be confused or associated with Lust for the former relates to incorporeal bodies whilst the latter to corporeal ones. The former is spiritual and the latter is ignorance. The former is immortal and the latter is changing. The former is enlightening and the latter is evil."

'With this Laozi had finished his speech and I started clapping to him taking the attention of the group towards me.' Alfred smiled for a moment and continued saying, 'I apologized to the group for eavesdropping on them and I praised Loazi for a wonderful speech. In response, Hermes invited me to join them and my workmate agreed to cover for me. Then, I thanked my workmate and joined the group. Before we continued with the remaining speeches, I introduced myself to the group and Plato introduced the group to me. He mentioned both of their real names and nicknames which I found a little hilarious at the time.

'Afterward, Plato started speaking his thoughts on Love saying, "Every soul is incomplete by nature. Every soul is partial, or not whole. That is, of course, when it is all alone, a soul feels emptiness inside of it. It is also compelled by its nature to seek out and fill that emptiness in order to become complete and whole. A good question to be asked here is, what completes a soul?

"In order to answer that question, we need to see how partials and fragments get created in the first place. A whole is a complete thing that, if it were ever divided, would leave out parts of it. Also, a whole has one nature to it that will be passed down to all the parts unchanged. Knowing this, let's examine the following argument. A fragment is a part of a whole, a whole is of one nature, and as the parts have that same nature as the whole, all of the parts of the same whole share the same nature. Apply the same logic and argument to souls. If a soul is a partial of a whole, then the only thing to unite with the soul, in order to make it whole again, is another soul.

"The next question to be answered now is which soul is fit enough or suitable to complete another soul? Continuing where Laozi has left off, I agree with him when he said that souls resonate in different frequencies, some in high frequencies and some in low ones, but, unfortunately, this is where my agreement ends. Souls do harmonize more with those which resonate closer to their own frequency, but it is not enough to fill that emptiness and make the incomplete whole again. The only possible way for a soul to be complete is by uniting with another soul that resonates in the same frequency as its own. Such souls are called soulmates.

"Some couples prefer to have similar hobbies and interests so that they get to practice them together and some couples prefer to have different hobbies and interests so that they get to teach each other, but, as for soulmates, these things are irrelevant to their relationship. To them, hobbies and interests fall under the criteria of choosing friends not lovers. What soulmates seek and find in their partner is a feeling of belonging to one another. A feeling of happiness resulting from the sole reason that their partner is part of their life. When two souls resonate in the same frequency, they are lost in true harmony and wonder. They complete each other and together they are whole again.

"Now, allow me to quote the philosopher Plato when he said in his Symposium, 'Love is the name for our pursuit of wholeness, for our desire to be complete.'"

"The philosopher Plato said it well and was directly to the point. When a soul searches for its soulmate, the soul that will complete it and make it whole, it searches for the feeling of love with, and towards, the other soul. And since Love happens only between soulmates, the search for the soulmate is the same as the search for Love. Thus, Love can be described as the pursuit of wholeness and as the desire to be complete, just like how the Philosopher Plato described it."

'With this Plato finished his speech,' said Alfred.

'That was delightful to hear,' I said.

'My thoughts exactly back then,' said Alfred. 'And now, after Plato, Hermes started his speech about Love saying, "Love occurs between two souls, one masculine and the other is feminine,' spoke Hermes. 'In order to understand the nature of this relation, we need to go all the way to the beginning, to the creation of the male and female souls. Let's start with a part Plato spoke about in his speech which is that each soul is a part of a whole. Now, parts are created by the division of a whole, and wholes precede parts in existence; therefore, regarding souls, they must originally have been created as a whole before getting divided into their individual parts of male and female. This being, which contains both aspects of male and female, is of androgynous nature.

"Now, let's examine the following two verses from the Holy Quran,

> "O mankind, fear you Lord, who created you from one soul and created from it its mate and dispersed from both of them many men and women. And fear Allah, through whom you ask one another, and the wombs. Indeed, Allah is ever, over you, an Observer." (The Holy Qur'an 4:1)

And,

> "And Allah has made for you from your soul mates and has made for you from your mates sons and grandchildren and has provided for you from the good things. Then in falsehood do they believe and in the favor of Allah they disbelieve." (The Holy Qur'an 16:72)

"The first verse speaks about the creation of all the souls of men and women and it goes as follows; it all started by the creation of the one original soul, then out of this soul its mate was created. Afterward, all of the rest of the souls were created from this pair of souls.

"The second verse speaks about the pattern and gender of creation of the other souls. Regarding the gender of the first two souls, since both of the souls and humans are the work of God, The Almighty, we can assume that the same pattern of creation that occurred to humans also occurred to souls. Thus, the first soul was androgynous in nature and out of it the feminine soul was created, or rather parted away from it, leaving the male part behind. Now, regarding the creation of the next generation of souls, the second verse states that it was through the female soul that male, and only male, souls were created. The verse then goes on to state that in the following generation, God has created for the original two souls, grandchildren souls. The use of the term 'grandchildren' and not 'grandsons' indicates that the genders of the souls that are in the grandchildren generation are both male and female in nature. This indicates that female souls were created even though they did not arise from the original female soul.

"All of these genders and generations might seem confusing so let's tie it all up. At first, an androgynous soul was created, then out of this soul its female part was created. Then, the female soul gave birth to androgynous souls as children. Afterwards, those androgynous souls went through the same process of division and giving birth that the first and second souls had gone through. And following this pattern of multiplication, all the rest of the souls were born.

"Let us now move on to the next step succeeding the creation of any pair of souls. In doing so, please pay close attention to the following excerpt from the Zohar,

> "When they first issue forth, they issue as male and
> female together. Subsequently, when they descend
> [to this world] they separate, one to one side and
> the other to the other, and God afterwards unites

them, God and no other. He alone knowing the mate proper to each. Happy the man who is upright in his works, or pure, and walks in the way of truth, so that his soul may find its original mate, for then he becomes indeed perfect, and through his perfection the whole world is blessed." (The Zohar)

"The Zohar clearly states that when the androgynous soul descends to the world, it splits into its male and female parts where each would be born into a physical body that matches their gender. The female and male souls don't have to descend to the world at the same time—there can be a gap of several years between each of them, and the male soul doesn't have to descend first before the female soul and vice versa. What is certain is that the split occurs when one of them is about to descend.

"Now, let us speak about the nature of the relationship between these two male and female souls that once have shared an androgynous spiritual body. Soulmates might be an appropriate term here, but it carries some inconsistency with what we said earlier about the creation of the male and female souls. Soulmates, as Plato said earlier, is a relation between two souls that resonate at the same frequency. And as Laozi said earlier, the resonance of a soul can be tuned via its actions. Therefore, the soulmate of a soul will not be constant along the years as both sides of the relationship will have their resonance changed a few times along the span of their lives.

"It was stated in the excerpts mentioned from the holy and sacred books, that soulmates, let's call them by that right now, have been decided from the moment they've been created. Meaning, there is only one fixed mate for each soul, not many or changing. These two male and female souls that have been whole once before are referred to by the esoteric name of Twin Flames.

"And now, let's divert our attention to how those twin flames reunite with each other. It is mentioned in the Talmud that;

Forty days prior to the formation of a child, a
heavenly voice cries out saying, "the daughter of
so and so is destined for so and so." (The Talmud
Sotah 2B)

This is, of course, the ideal case, but not every soul is fortunate to
meets its true other half. In the Zohar excerpt that I mentioned earlier, it
is stated that a man must live a pure and pious life so that God may reward
him by reuniting him with his actual other half. It is only logical that since
God is the one who created all of the androgynous souls, split those souls
into male and female parts, and put each one into a corresponding physical
body, that through him, and only him, the union of twin flames is ever possible. There is a saying for Prophet Mohammed, peace be upon him and his
family, that reads;

"No building has been built in Islam more beloved
to Allah Almighty than marriage."

Although many see that the saying refers to normal marriage, the
Arabic word used for 'marriage' has the same root as the word mentioned
in the Qur'anic verse for 'mates'. Thus, the marriage mentioned in the saying
can also be interpreted as referring to the union of twin flames.

"Regarding the relationship between twin flames, Love is seen to be
all that relationship is about. The seeking of Love is the seeking for one's true
other half and the recognition of Love is the recognition of that half as well.
In the philosopher Plato's *Symposium*, regarding the yearning for the other
flame, we read:

"Love is born into every human being; it calls back
the halves of our original nature together. It tries to
make one out of two and heal the wound of human
nature." (The Symposium)

Also, in the *Symposium*, regarding the union of twin flames, we read:

"And so, when a person meets the half that is his
very own, whatever his orientation, whether it's
to young men or not, then something wonderful
happens; the two are struck from their senses by
love, by a sense of belonging to one another, and by
desire, and they don't want to be separated from one
another, not even for a moment." (The Symposium)

"Continuing with the journey of the twin flames, we arrive now to the
kind of life that united, or married, twin flames have. Let's see what God has
bestowed upon them in the following qur'anic verse;

"And of His signs is that he created for you, from
yourselves mates that you may find tranquility in
them; and He placed between you intimacy and
mercy. Indeed in that are signs for a people who
give thought." (The Holy Qur'an 30:21)

"The relationship that takes place between twin flames is of the purest
kind of all and through them that true Love is ever found, felt, and experienced. Love is the greatest gift of God to those who have stood upright against
the temptations of life. Wicked souls get lost in lust thinking they have found
love but it is a far cry from them. Good souls get rewarded with good souls
but not necessarily their twin flames. Only pious souls get reunited with their
original halves and are rewarded with Love.

"The things to say about twin flames and love are endless, some we
have no time for right now and some are beyond the comprehension of the
simple human mind. Therefore, I will conclude my speech about Love with
a quote from the philosopher Plato from his *Symposium*, his magnum opus
on Love, in which he said;

"Ancient is the desire of one another which is
implanted in us, reuniting our original nature,
making one of two, and healing the state of man.

Each of us when separated, having one side only, like a flat fish, is but the indentation of a man, and he is always looking for his other half. When one of them meets with his other half, the actual half of himself, the pair are lost in an amazement of love, friendship, and intimacy.

"These are the people who pass their whole lives together; yet they could not explain what they desire of one another. For the intense yearning which each of them has towards the other does not appear to be the desire of lover's intercourse, but of something else which the soul of either evidently desires and cannot tell." (The Symposium)

'And thus, Hermes finished his speech about love.' Alfred then took a sip of tea and continued, 'Now, it was the time for the last speech, that of Luqman's who started with, "There is no doubt that the twin-flame relationship that Hermes mentioned is of the highest, if not the very highest, relationships that can occur between souls, but we must not be too eager to associate that kind of relationship with Love, at least to the way we assume it to be. It is necessary, in order to understand anything, to go back and examine its origin. Therefore, we must look into what the creator of Love, God the Almighty, has to say about it.

"Let's start with the quotes that Hermes mentioned in his speech and reflect upon them. But before we start, since we want to know God's point of view on the matter, we should only examine the quotes taken from the Holy Quran and the Zohar for the former is the word of God, whilst the latter is a commentary on the word of God, the Torah. As for the quotes made by the philosopher Plato, we must leave them out of the examination—not for the reason that Plato is wrong, but for the reason that Plato's words are not those of God and, as wise as he was, he could still be wrong about the matter of Love.

"If we reflect on the quotes from the Holy Quran and the Zohar, we see that they speak about the creation of the first androgynous soul and its multiplication. We also see the creation of twin flames, their descent, and how they are reunited with each other. As for the relation between twin flames, let's examine the follow qur'anic verse thoroughly;

> "And of His signs is that he created for you, from yourselves mates that you may find tranquility in them; and He placed between you intimacy and mercy. Indeed in that are signs for a people who give thought." (The Holy Qur'an 30:21)

The verse speaks about the kind of emotions that God bestowed upon twin flames, which are tranquility, intimacy, and mercy. If we look carefully at the verse, we'd see that Love is nowhere to be found. It is not a fault that a great emotion such as Love cannot be found among the greatest relationship between souls, which is that of twin flames, but it is by design. Then, if it is so, where could Love be?

"A story worth mentioning here is that of Jacob and an angel. During the last year of the drought that hit the land, after Jacob had gone blind, an angel visited Jacob and asked him of the reason behind his blindness. Jacob said that the sadness of losing his son, Joseph, who he loved most in his heart, had caused his blindness.

In reply, the angel said to Jacob, "The heart is the sanctuary of God, so don't accommodate in his sanctuary another beside him."

The angel then said, "Your God is a jealous God, and the heart cannot accommodate two lovers."

Afterwards, Jacob realized his mistake of having another being in his heart besides God and so he repented and God reunited him with his son Joseph as a reward.

"The previous story teaches that the heart is the sanctuary of loved ones and thus the dwelling place of Love itself. It also teaches that Love can be given to only one person and no heart can accommodate two lovers. Thus, if someone lay claim to loving two things or two people, he is either a liar or a fooled one, because, since the heart can accommodate one only, one of the two things or persons must leave while the other dwells. The last thing taught by the story is that God is a participant in this equation that involves the heart and Love.

"Since the heart is claimed by God as his sanctuary, and Love dwells only in the heart, and since God doesn't accept to be a partner of or be partnered with anything or anyone, specified by his jealousy, Love is therefore a matter relating to God who won't accept it if it wasn't exclusively dedicated to him. And if Love is associated with God, it surely must be divine in essence.

"This is the true divine Love, loving God, which cannot be achieved other than renouncing the love of everything and anyone, no matter how dear it is to the heart, and devoting all of the love to God the Almighty alone. Also know this: in order to love God, you need to be loved by him initially, thus, one must seek the love of God primarily and earn it worthily. So, how is God's love earned?

"To be loved by God, one must earn his satisfaction first. And God's satisfaction is earned by being pious, doing what pleases God and averting from what discontents him, and by being satisfied with God's decree, whether it is good or evil. Once God's satisfaction is earned, one will be receptible of God's love. Later, when God starts loving a person, the love of God will start to fill the heart of that person until it takes domain over all of it. And when the heart is filled with love devoted exclusively to God, true divine Love will be achieved and felt.

"Once a person becomes immersed in the love of God, he will revert from anything that would keep him busy from God. He will see the world in the eyes of his beloved Lord. Anything that God loves, he will love and cherish, and anything that God hates he will hate and despise. When the prophet Mohammed, peace be upon him and his family, ascended to the empyrean heaven, he spoke to Allah, or God, from behind the empyrean fiery veils. The conversation is long, but I'd like to mention a segment of it that relates to our topic.

The Prophet asked God, "Oh my lord, I would like to know who do you love from your servants so that I love him."

God replied, "If you see my servant mentioning me a lot, then I have given him permission to do so and I love him. And if you see my servant not mentioning me, then I have veiled him and I hate him."

"And once God loves a person, he inspires him with obedience, compels him with contentment, gives him understanding of religion, and strengthens him with certainty, then he, the servant, is satisfied with self-sufficiency and clothed with chastity. And if God hates a person, he adores money to him and bestows it for him, inspires him in his worldly life, and entrusts him to his desires, and then the person rides stubbornness, spread corruption, and oppresses other people.

"Those who devote their love and hearts to God alone don't stop loving other things; instead, the love of God is branchable and able to contain everything but under few rules. God's obedience is the main rule, it is the only rule, a devotee will love anything and anyone that will help him keep and strive after that rule and would hate anything and anyone that goes against it. Who is loving in God, is loving God, and who is loved in God, is a lover of God; all of that is because they don't ever love except in God."

'And so, the last speech ended.' Alfred then got lost in his memories with a smile on his face. I recognized his smile being of someone remembering something beautiful and so I stayed silent and didn't interrupt his thoughts. 'Anyway, how did you find the topic and the speeches?' asked Alfred after a while.

'The topic was very interesting and the speeches were pleasing to hear,' I said. 'To be honest, even though every speech was different than the others, each one of them was beautiful and true in its own way.'

'I agree with you on that,' said Alfred.

'There is one more thing that I want you to tell me,' I said.

'Sure, what is it?' replied Alfred.

'You said, while recalling the story, Plato introduced the group to you by their real names, right?' I said.

'That is correct,' replied Alfred.

'Can you tell me their real names, please?' I pleaded

Alfred then looked at this wrist watch and said, 'Would you look at the time! My break is over. I need to get back to work.'

'You're not even on a break!' I said.

Alfred laughed cunningly as he left the table. I meant to stop him right then, but the way he left made me laugh and unable to speak, and because of that, he got away from me.

After my laughter ended, I used the quietness around me to reflect on the story Alfred had just told me. What a wonderful story it really was. What I found most captivating about it was that each of the four speeches was different from the others and yet beautiful in its own way. They were examples of a true beauty in diverse opinions, visions, and beliefs. Something else that I also found admirable was how they had their conversation even though they had different and opposing opinions about Love. This is how a conversation should unfold. Differences of opinions shouldn't spoil etiquette between people.

CHAPTER 9

Personality Traits

I was sitting alone at one of the outdoor tables of the café. I'd been waiting for about an hour to see if Plato or any of his friends would show up, but still no one did.

'I really hate not doing something,' I spoke to myself whilst playing with my empty café cup. 'It is so boring when no one is around.'

Then Alfred came to me and said, 'You look very bored, what's wrong?'

'Hi, Alfred,' I replied with a yawn. 'It is as you said, I'm bored because no one is here today.'

Alfred laughed as he collected my café cup.

'By the way, Alfred,' I said, 'do Plato and his friend run into this situation?'

'What do you mean?' asked Alfred.

'I mean, when they come and don't find each other,' I replied.

'Of course, it happens sometimes,' Alfred said.

'What do they do in such cases? How do they keep themselves occupied?' I said.

'Some bring a book to read with them,' said Alfred, 'some use their mobile phones, and some just get lost in their own thoughts.'

Then, a scene happening outside the café caught my and Alfred's attention. There was a man sitting in one of the café tables in the outdoor that was approached by a child beggar. The child was talking to the man who didn't pay the child any attention and kept drinking his coffee and using his phone as if no one was talking to him. After a minute, the child gave up and left with a sad face.

'What a miserly man!' I said to Alfred. 'He didn't say anything to the poor child. He didn't even look at him. If you don't want to give money, no one is forcing you. Just don't treat the child that way. He was so miser and rude.'

Alfred looked at me for a moment and then said, 'My break is about to start; do you mind if I spent it with you?'

'No, not at all,' I replied gladly.

'I'll be right back,' said Alfred.

After a while, Alfred came and he brought with him a teapot and two cups. He put the tray on the table and when he was about to start pouring the tea, I took the pot and poured for the both of us. Alfred smiled and sat down.

'How are you today, Nate?' asked Alfred.

'I'm fine, what about you?' I responded.

'Pretty good, all thanks to God,' replied Alfred. 'How do you like the group so far?'

'I like them very much,' I said. 'I feel lucky to be their friend.'

'And how do you find the conversations?' asked Alfred.

'Very beautiful and interesting. Beautiful in their execution and interesting in their logic and reasoning,' I answered.

'Splendid!' said Alfred. 'How about we have a conversation of our own?'

'I'd love to,' I said with little doubt that someone like Alfred would be able to make and hold a conversation similar to those of Plato and his friends.

Either way, I saw it as a great opportunity to test myself at a conversation and see how much I had improved.

'A few minutes ago, you called that person a miser, right?' said Alfred.

'Yes, I did,' I replied, a little confused by Alfred's opening.

'Why did you call him that?' asked Alfred.

'Because he refused to give the child his attention and money,' I replied.

'Let me ask you this, what is a miser?' said Alfred.

'The desire to accumulate wealth and the hatred to spend it on others,' I said.

'I didn't mean *what does it mean*,' said Alfred. 'I meant *what is it?*'

'I don't get you,' I replied.

'Isn't being a miser a personality trait?' said Alfred.

'Yes, it is,' I replied.

'And by saying that the person is miserly, aren't you implying that he is a holder of that trait?' said Alfred.

'Necessarily,' I replied.

My reply made Alfred smile and I asked why. 'You said "necessarily,"' said Alfred. 'You are starting to speak like the group.' Alfred and I started laughing. 'Let's get back to the topic,' Alfred continued. 'My question here is, how does someone gain or acquire a personality trait?'

'That's an interesting question,' I remarked.

'But before that, we need to define what a personality trait is,' said Alfred.

I answered with, 'I would say that it is a distinctive quality or a characteristic belonging to a person.'

'That is correct,' said Alfred. 'Now, how does someone acquire a trait?'

'Impressions,' I said, 'I think having an impression of a trait can be a sign of it.'

'Interesting answer,' said Alfred. 'It is true that sometimes impressions of traits can be signs of people having those traits, but is this always the case? Don't you sometimes get an impression of a stranger only to be proven wrong?

'As a matter of fact,' I spoke, 'it happens a lot and I don't understand why people who have the impression of being something good can turn out to have the opposite trait.'

'So, impressions can't be how one acquires a trait,' said Alfred.

'What about what causes impressions in the first place?' I said.

'What do you mean?' asked Alfred.

'I mean actions,' I explained. 'You sometimes get an impression of a person by seeing him perform an action, right?'

'Yes,' Alfred replied.

'So, actions lead to impressions, right?' I said, feeling a little happy that I was leading the conversation.

'Yes,' said Alfred.

I said, 'If one's action gives the impression of a trait and a simple, or a one-time impression is not enough for someone to acquire a trait, how about the repetitiveness of an action? Wouldn't that be an indicator for an acquired trait?'

'Let us examine your statement,' said Alfred. 'You said that actions lead to impressions and impressions lead to traits. You're implying that traits are the cause of the actions. I would agree with that, for actions are based on, and manifest from, the traits and that's how traits are known.'

'Seems reasonable,' I commented.

'Impressions are a good point when it comes to how traits are known to others,' said Alfred, 'but when it comes to how traits are acquired? There is a serious problem with them.'

'What is that problem?' I asked.

'Impressions are personal,' spoke Alfred, 'in which they will differ from one person to another. And let us not forget that the person seeing the actions of others is interpreting them based on his own feelings, meanings, and beliefs. For example, one action by a person might be understood and interpreted differently by two people, is this not correct?'

'Yes, it is,' I replied.

'If impressions are begotten this way, they are subjective, right?' said Alfred.

'Yes, they are,' I replied.

'And subjectivity can hold many things at the same time, agreeing and opposing, right?' said Alfred.

'Correct,' I said.

'So, through subjectivity one cannot find a definitive answer,' said Alfred. 'We need to look elsewhere to find out how traits are required.'

'What about the objective side of actions?' I said. 'Let's leave impressions aside and see which traits an action expresses. If an action gets repeated a lot, can't it be a sign of acquiring the trait it expresses or prompts?'

'Someone with a trait will always behave or act according to that trait to a certain degree,' said Alfred, 'But he may not always act according to that trait in all situations and circumstances.'

'I don't understand,' I said.

'Take, for example, the following three fathers all with multiple children.' Alfred continued, 'The first father is generous only with one of his children. The second father is generous with all of his children, but he is not generous with strangers. The third father is generous with all, children and strangers alike. Now, which one of these three fathers would you say has acquired the trait of generosity?'

'Well, let's see,' I spoke, 'I wouldn't call the first father generous, for he who favors a child among the others is something else. As for the two remaining fathers, I would say that they are both generous ,but the third father is more generous than the second one.'

'Concerning the second father,' said Alfred, 'when it comes to giving money or charity to strangers, would he do it?'

'No, he wouldn't,' I replied.

'So then in that situation, what kind of trait will he be displaying, that of generosity or that of miserliness?' asked Alfred.

'Of course, that of miserliness,' I answered.

'Now the father will be holding two traits at the same time, right?' said Alfred.

'It appears so,' I said, confused.

'Is that possible?' asked Alfred.

I thought that I had fallen into some kind of a trap or a trick and I answered, not out of my belief, but to what I thought Alfred would think was correct. 'It shouldn't be; I don't think someone can have two opposing traits at the same time.'

'Why not?' responded Alfred.

Alfred's response made me more confused and I replied with, 'Because two opposing things can't coexist in the same medium or thing.'

'Is that so?' started Alfred. 'Let us reflect on cold and hot or heat. They are two opposing degrees of the same nature, that is temperature, which is in everything. There is nothing without a temperature degree that can either be closer to the heat end or that of cold.

'Cold and heat lie on opposing ends of the scale of temperature and their meeting point or the midpoint of the temperature spectrum is what we call *warmth*. Now, let me ask you this, to which end does *warmth* belong, to that of cold or that of heat?'

I thought for a moment and answered, 'Since it is in the midpoint between cold and heat, I don't think it is wise to associate it solely with one of them.'

'Very wise indeed.' Alfred's response made me smile. 'Warmth is the result of both cold and heat, and because of that we can't associate it only with one of them. Following this premise, can we say that warmth consists of cold and heat?'

'Yes, we can,' I said.

'Can you figure out which part makes the most out of warmth?' said Alfred.

'We agreed that warmth is in the center of the temperature scale,' I said, 'so, I would say that warmth consists of equal parts of cold and heat. Like 50% cold and 50% heat.'

'I like how you used percentages in your answer,' said Alfred. 'Warmth has also a range in which it is sometimes closer to the heat pole and sometimes closer to the cold pole. Do you think this is possible?'

'Yes, I do,' I replied.

'Let's take a drink, for example, and assume that the warmth degree of it is a little bit closer to the heat pole,' said Alfred. 'How would you distribute the percentages of cold and heat then?'

'Something like 40% cold and 60% heat,' I replied.

'Now, does the drink consist of both cold and heat or does it only consist of heat since it has the higher percentage?' asked Alfred.

'I would say both, for even if heat has the higher percentage that doesn't mean that cold ceased to exist,' I answered.

'Very good. Now, let us summarize quickly,' spoke Alfred. 'Cold and heat are of the same nature but of different opposing degrees. They can co-exist together in objects even in different degrees or percentages. Let's take this thought process and apply it to personality traits.

'Just like cold and heat, traits also come in pairs such as: mercy and ruthlessness, weakness and strength, and in our example earlier, generosity and miserliness. They are all different degrees of the same natures. A person can't have one trait in him without having the opposite one as well at the same time. All people have all kinds of personality traits, but they differ only in the percentages or shares of the opposing traits. What do you think?'

'I totally agree with you,' I replied, amazed by Alfred's statement. 'But following your statement, it means that all traits are self-acquired, and hence, one cannot acquire a trait because he already has it, right?'

'No, not at all,' replied Alfred. 'What is self-acquired are the natures of the traits but not the traits themselves.'

'I'm a little bit confused,' I said. 'Wouldn't acquiring the nature mean acquiring its traits by default?'

'Not necessarily,' said Alfred. 'Acquiring a nature means having the potentiality or the possibility of acquiring either of its two traits.' Alfred noticed my confused face, smiled, and then continued, 'Let me clarify: it is true that having a nature means having its traits, but what we want to know is when does someone become associated with only one trait out of the two, for only then can we say that a trait has been acquired.'

'I understand now,' I said.

'Let's rephrase the main question to, when does someone truly acquire a trait?' said Alfred. 'When does someone deserve to be called by a trait?'

'Let's see,' I spoke, 'the midpoint between two traits consists equally of 50% of each trait. And an increase in the percentage of any trait will result in it having the majority of the percentage. So, can it be that one acquires a trait when he has the majority of the percentage in it?'

'Before I answer your question,' said Alfred, 'let's continue with the example of generosity and miserliness for an easier conversation.'

'I agree with that,' I replied.

'So, according to your suggestion,' Alfred continued, 'if someone's actions are more generous than miserly, you would call him a generous man.'

'Yes,' I replied.

'Even if it was only 51%?' asked Alfred.

'Maybe not 51%, for this is too close to the midpoint,' I answered, 'but more like 60%.'

'Let's examine this hypothetical person who is 60% generous and 40% miserly,' said Alfred. 'The majority of his actions are generous, but still, he has a lot of miser in him. He cannot acquire the trait yet, for this contradicts our earlier premise that one must be associated only with one trait. In our example, the person is still both generous and miserly.

'The only way to have one trait is for that trait to dominate, so to speak, its opposite pair. And that will happen only when a trait reaches the 100% mark leaving the other with 0% or nothing.'

'But based on the premise,' I said, 'to be associated only with one trait is to have it at 100% and this can't be the case.'

'Why not?' asked Alfred.

'A person can't achieve 100% of a trait,' I said, 'it is impossible to do that. Thus, I would say that 80% of a trait shall be enough to acquire it.'

'How would you measure percentages?' Alfred continued. 'How do you know that someone has reached the 80% mark and now he has acquired a trait?'

'I don't think there is a way for an exact measurement,' I said, 'but what about the high frequency of the actions related to the trait; wouldn't that be an indicator of high percentage?'

'High frequency might truly lead to a high percentage, but following this logic, we will have another problem at our hand,' Alfred continued. 'When you say that 80% is enough to acquire the positive trait, assuming you are desiring the positive one, you are also justifying having a bit of the negative one.

'With this premise in action, people's wrongdoings can be excused as being that of the justified margin of the negative trait and the goal of completing the positive trait will seem meaningless and will be lost.'

'That is true,' I said, 'but the same can be said about your statement. How would you know that someone has reached the 100% mark with a trait if it can't be measured?'

'Percentages less than 100% can't be measured, regarding personality traits, but the 100% mark can be,' said Alfred.

'How so?' I asked.

Alfred answered, 'When a trait reaches 100%, what percentage will its counter pair be at?'

'It will be at 0%,' I replied.

'And when a trait is at 0% in a person, will it manifest in his actions or be absent from them?' said Alfred.

'It will be absent,' I replied.

'Therefore, the absence of one trait means the 100% completion or presence of its opposite trait, right?' said Alfred.

'Yes, it is,' I replied.

'Well, here is our way of measurement,' said Alfred.

'One thing I still don't understand,' I spoke, 'is how would knowing the percentage of a trait help in answering our revised question of how a trait is truly acquired?'

Alfred replied saying, 'We concluded earlier that every nature has two opposing traits associated with it that are different in degrees, right?'

'Yes,' I replied.

Alfred continued, 'We also agreed on the premise that one must be associated only with one trait in order to truly acquire it, right?'

'Yes, we did,' I replied.

'Let us now go back to our example of cold and heat,' said Alfred. 'If we give random percentages of cold and heat to water per se, aren't we referring to the compositional percentages of cold and heat?'

'Yes, we are,' I replied.

'Meaning that the water has both traits of cold and heat?' said Alfred.

'Supposedly,' I replied.

Alfred continued, 'What about if the water reached the freezing point—how would you distribute the percentages of cold and heat temperatures at that point?'

'I would say that cold is 100% and heat is 0%,' I replied.

Alfred continued, 'What about if the water reached the boiling point?'

'In this case, heat will be 100% and cold 0%,' I replied.

Alfred continued, 'In the previous two examples, was the water associated with two traits or only one trait at the same time?'

I smiled at the conclusion and said, 'It was associated with only one trait.'

'How did the water get associated with one trait only?' asked Alfred.

I answered uncertainly, saying, 'When the other trait reached 0%?'

'Exactly,' replied Alfred. 'And when a trait reaches 0% share, it ceases to exist, right?'

'I believe so,' I said.

'Isn't this the state that we are looking for?' said Alfred.

'Yes, it is,' I replied.

'Going back to our example of generosity and miserliness,' said Alfred. 'One must relinquish all habits and behaviors of being a miser to truly be generous and acquire the trait of generosity.'

'I get it now,' I said. 'I think we have arrived to our answer. It is through the abandonment of one trait that its pair is acquired, right?'

'We shouldn't be too hasty in claiming victory over the matter,' said Alfred. 'We need to examine the matter at hand from all directions and angles.'

'What is left to examine?' I asked, confused.

'Sustainability,' answered Alfred.

'What do you mean?' I said.

'I mean the ability to sustain a trait at 100% no matter the costs, situations, and circumstances.'

'I still don't understand you,' I replied.

'Let us examine the following example,' spoke Alfred. 'Take two persons both with 100% generosity. The only difference between them is that while facing personal problems or difficult circumstances and their generosity is put to the test, one will stay at 100% no matter what and perform the generous act while the other won't sustain the 100% and will not perform the generous act at that time.

'Knowing that the second person would later, after his hardship is over, get back to his 100% state, which of the two persons would you say is truly generous?'

I took a moment to contemplate Alfred's example and then replied, 'This is one hard question. I know that the first person is much better than the second one for he was able to stay generous throughout his problems, but in the same time, I can't bring myself to accuse the second person of not being generous just because he was having a hard situation, especially considering the fact that he has achieved 100% of the generosity trait.'

'You are thinking subjectively,' said Alfred. 'We must leave subjectivity behind us and examine the matter through objectivity so there will be no place for doubt of falseness. Subjectivity carries with it right and wrong at the same time, therefore, we can't judge something subjective. We need to know objectively how a trait is truly acquired, regardless of feelings or what we think and assume to be possible or not.'

'All right,' I said. 'But I still believe that both persons are generous.'

'In that case,' Alfred continued, 'let's examine the two persons against the premise of the way to truly acquire a trait which is through being associated only, and we might add always, with one trait.

'The first person has achieved 100% completion in the generosity trait and in difficult circumstances, he is able to sustain his generosity and do the generous act. Such a person has abandoned the opposite trait and no matter what the circumstance is, he sustains his generosity. Is this person compliant with our premise or not?'

'Yes, he is,' I replied.

'The second person, on the other hand,' spoke Alfred, 'has achieved 100% in the generosity trait but in difficult circumstances, he doesn't sustain his generosity. Such person reverts back to the opposite traits in certain circumstances. Is this person compliant with our premise or not?'

'No, he is not,' I said.

'Now, out of the two persons, who do you think has truly acquired the trait in accordance with the premise?' said Alfred.

'The first one of course,' I replied.

'You see, it is not enough to complete 100% in a trait; to truly acquire it, one needs also to sustain the trait no matter the circumstances.' Alfred continued, 'To truly be deserving to be called and known by a trait is no easy task. It requires a strong will and determination against life and its problems. One truly with a trait doesn't differentiate between kin and a stranger or a friend and a foe. He treats all people equally, according to his own traits and manners, not with those of other people—whether the person wronged him or made good to him, that doesn't matter.

'Such a person is strong and stable against what life brings. He is like a mountain that doesn't bow, no matter how strong the winds blowing against him are. He sticks to his traits no matter what, even if all people and circumstances are against him.

'Such a person has truly acquired and is fully associated with a trait. He is worthy to carry its title and be known by it.'

'That was fascinating, Alfred!' I said. I was really amazed by his statement. I never thought that Alfred could make an argument as strong as that of Plato and his friends.

'Thank you, Nate,' Alfred replied with a smile.

'I think we have arrived to our answer and the end of this lovely conversation,' I said.

'It is true that we have arrived at a satisfying answer,' replied Alfred, 'but our conversation is far from over.'

'What is left to discuss?' I asked.

'What is left is the reason why we had this conversation in the first place,' answered Alfred.

'Didn't we start the conversation to see how a trait is acquired?' I said.

'No, it was just a means to an end,' Alfred replied.

'What end are you speaking about?' I said.

'Tell me, why do we seek knowledge?' said Alfred.

'To get knowledge and not to be ignorant,' I replied.

'That is the first step; what's the next one?' asked Alfred.

I thought about it for a moment and replied with, 'I don't know.'

'We seek knowledge in various fields of life so that we may use and apply that knowledge, don't we?' said Alfred.

'Yes, I believe so,' I replied.

'Now, since we have sought and obtained the knowledge of how traits are acquired,' said Alfred, 'we need to know how to use that knowledge, don't we?'

'Supposedly, but how?' I asked.

'Let me address you directly from now on,' started Alfred. 'I taught you how traits are acquired so that you would apply this knowledge into your own life and strive honestly after the positive traits or manners. I taught you how hard it is to truly acquire a trait so that you won't fool yourself thinking that you have acquired a one just because few of your actions resemble that trait.

Use this knowledge to better yourself and be honest with yourself against all difficult odds.'

The way Alfred was advising me reminded me of my grandfather and how he would speak to me, with the love and care that a father would show to his son.

And so, I felt that Alfred was speaking to me from the bottom of his heart and his words had touched mine. It was such an amazing feeling that I couldn't find the words to say back to him that would do him justice and I stayed silent. But deep down inside my heart, Alfred started holding a special place.

'Until now we've been speaking about acquiring the good, or positive traits, but don't forget that it goes both ways,' said Alfred.

'What do you mean?' I asked.

Alfred answered with, 'I mean that, as it is hard for someone to acquire a positive trait, it is also as hard to acquire the negative one. A person needs to be 100% on the negative trait to truly be deserving of being called by that trait.'

'That is true,' I said.

'Which brings us now to you,' said Alfred.

'Me?!' I said, really confused.

'Yes, you.' Alfred continued, 'Earlier today, we saw a man that refused to give charity to a child beggar and you called him a miser. You don't know the man and yet you saw he was deserving to be called miser.'

'You are right,' I said. 'But a question that comes to mind is, if one is not deserving to be called by a trait till he achieves 100% in it, which is uncommon, how am I to describe people then?'

'You describe their actions instead,' said Alfred. 'We agreed that the positive trait and its negative counterpart are different degrees of the same nature, right?'

'Yes,' I replied.

'And since they lie on the same scale,' Alfred continued, 'one can move to either trait, right?'

'Yes,' I replied.

'Which, in turn, means that one can change from one trait to the other?' said Alfred.

'Yes, I believe so,' I replied.

Alfred continued, 'And we ought to change ourselves towards the positive traits and help change others as well.'

'Correct,' I replied.

'That's why it is necessary to describe people's actions instead of themselves,' Alfred continued. 'When you accuse someone of a negative trait, it becomes hard for him to change as this will create a defensive barrier within himself. But if you describe a person's action instead, it is easier for him to change as he won't see himself as the suspect of a bad trait.'

'I totally agree with that,' I said. 'To be honest, I see this happening to me. Sometimes when someone accuses me of a bad thing, I look past the fact that the other person actually wants to help me change for the better and get stuck at, that if I agree to change, I will confirm that I have a bad thing in me.'

'I'm glad you understand this point,' said Alfred with a smile.

'Believe me, I do!' I replied.

Alfred then looked at his watch and said, 'I'm afraid my breaktime is over. Before I get back to work, let me tell you this advice.'

'What is it?' I said.

'It is about thinking the best of people, especially strangers,' spoke Alfred. 'Whenever you meet new people, always assume the best of them and that they have acquired all of the positive traits until their actions prove otherwise.' Then Alfred stood up and looked at me in a funny way and said, 'With these kinds of people walking around, trust me, you don't have to wait that much till they do prove otherwise.'

Alfred's way of saying his last phrase where he widened his eyes and raised his eyebrows made me smile.

'See you around, kid!' said Alfred as he left to enter the café.

Speaking with Alfred had clarified something for me. Before, I had an unsettled doubt about perfection and if it should be sought after, but now I've learned that striving after perfection in a trait, or anything else, is the only way to achieve things. If you settle for low standards, you will never truly attain anything. Standards need to be at the level of perfection so that pursuers can really achieve the thing they're seeking after.

Also, at the beginning, I had my own doubts about Alfred and his ability to hold a strong conversation. I judged him based on his occupation and not as a person. And to be honest, he had proven himself to be as wise as Plato himself, if not wiser. He had truly shown me that anyone can be a philosopher and that Wisdom is not relegated to a particular type of people. And after that day, I had so much respect for him.

CHAPTER 10

Logic

The next day, I received a text from Plato informing me about a gathering happening that night at an hour much later than usual to the group. As I would never miss a discussion, especially one where the group agreed beforehand to meet—which usually meant an important topic.

I reached the café at the agreed upon time and as I was entering the café, I noticed Luqman sitting alone at one of the outside tables. I went to him, exchanged greetings, and joined his table.

'Tonight's weather is very nice, isn't it?' I said. There was a gentle breeze that filled the air bringing a little chill.

'I was going to sit inside initially, but after I saw the weather outside and how nice it is, I couldn't resist,' said Luqman.

'Hey, Luqman, can I ask you a question?' I said.

'Sure,' Luqman replied.

'Where are you and the rest of the group from?' I asked. 'Not all of you strike me as being from Paris, if you don't mind me asking.'

'No, not at all,' spoke Luqman. 'I am from Saudi Arabia. Plato is from Greece. Protagoras is from… Italy, if I'm not mistaken. While Hypatia and Alfred are from Paris.'

'Wow! Everyone is from a different country,' I said.

'And little Nate is from America,' added Luqman with a smile.

I smiled, then replied saying, 'What's tonight's topic, anyway?'

'Don't be hasty, you'll find out soon enough,' said Luqman.

After that, I glanced over and saw Plato about to enter the café and I said to Luqman nodding at Plato, 'Look, isn't that Plato sitting over there?'

Luqman looked at Plato and said, 'Yes, indeed. He thinks we're inside. We better call.' Luqman then raised his hand and called for Plato, grabbing his attention.

Afterward, Plato came and joined our table.

'It's a good thing you and Nate are here. Let's order something now while we wait for the others,' said Plato.

'Hypatia and Protagoras texted me earlier,' said Luqman, 'they won't be able to come tonight.'

'That is unfortunate. I guess we'll have to proceed without them then,' replied Plato.

Then, Alfred approached us and said, 'Good evening, gentlemen.'

'Good evening, Alfred,' Plato replied.

'My shift just ended. I hope I can join you tonight if that's not too much to ask?' said Alfred.

'That's nonsense, you know you're always welcome, Alfred!' replied Plato.

'Thank you,' said Alfred as he took a seat at our table.

I was a little sad when Luqman informed us that neither Protagoras nor Hypatia would be coming tonight, but when Alfred joined us, I became very excited to see what kind of discussion would unfold. It was the first time to see Alfred in a discussion with the group.

Afterwards, everyone ordered his choice of coffee that would help him stay focused at night and we delved into the conversation.

'So, what's the topic for tonight?' asked Alfred.

'Tonight's topic is Logic,' answered Luqman.

'Logic, that seems interesting,' said Alfred.

'My thoughts exactly!' I said to myself.

'There is no doubt that all of you have heard about logic many times,' Plato began, 'and heard people speaking about speeches being logical or illogical even more times. But what exactly is logic? I think it is about time that we sat together and discussed this.'

'That we must,' said Alfred, 'you have no idea how many times I had to listen to some people's nonsense and hear them say it is logical.'

Plato smiled and said, 'Before we try and define what logic is, let us first see its features and the things logic is associated with.'

'Why don't we start by seeing where logic is applicable or used,' said Alfred, 'or what parts of speech is it involved in?'

'I see Logic as involved in speeches that consist of premises, arguments, and conclusions,' said Plato.

'That's a good start. Would you care to elaborate more?' said Alfred.

'With pleasure,' started Plato. 'Premises are the building blocks for an argument which the argumentator believes to be true, logical, or both. The conclusion is the final statement that is desired to be proven by the argument. It is the result of the argument made.

'As for the argument, it is the core of this three-part structure. It is the method of sewing together the premises to deduce the conclusion statement. It is just like if the premises were dots, and the way to connect those dots is the argument; connecting all the dots draws the bigger picture, which is the conclusion.'

'Well said, Plato' said Alfred. 'I want to linger more on the argument part and examine it further, as I see it as the most important part of the structure.'

'I agree,' said Plato. 'Why don't we start by seeing what the function of an argument is?'

'When you have a couple of facts and you want to prove a certain conclusion,' spoke Alfred, 'the argument will be the proof needed to prove the conclusion.'

'How can an argument be a proof?' asked Plato.

'An argument is driven from the premises it is based upon,' said Alfred. 'It uses those premises to reason a conclusion. This reasoning provides the proof for that conclusion.'

'I understand now,' said Plato. 'So, the function of an argument is reasoning, correct?'

'Correct, if you oversimplify it, but I can go into more beneficial details to see how reasoning is carried out,' said Alfred.

'Please do,' replied Plato.

'Before you continue, Alfred, and sorry to interrupt you,' I spoke, 'could you please explain to me what you mean by a premise statement?'

'Premise statements hold the information you want to use to prove your conclusion,' said Alfred. 'An example argument will go like this: because of A and B, C is like this. Here A and B will be your premise statements used to prove the conclusion statement of C. Is it clear now?'

'Yes, crystal clear,' I replied.

'When we use words such as premises and conclusions,' Alfred continued, 'we draw the argument in a forward-thinking way which tends to overlook the position of what is to be proved from the whole argument.

Let's use the following words instead. Let's substitute premises with facts and presumptions, and substitute conclusions with results.

'With those new words the structure will be: facts or presumptions, arguments, and results. So far, the method of argumentation we used is one where we see what facts and presumptions are available and deduce a conclusion from them. This argumentative method is called deduction. In this method, facts are known while the result is unknown and must be figured out through deduction. The flow of this method will go as follows: facts to deduction to result.

An example of the deduction method will be as follows:

- If you see a big fire, this will be your fact.

- And knowing that fire eats everything it touches will be your argument.

- A large pile of burned things and ashes will be your deduced conclusion

'There is another argumentative method where the flow is opposite to that of the deduction method and it goes like this: results to argument to facts or presumptions. In this method, the result is known while the facts and the presumptions are unknown and must be discovered. This argumentative method is called "inference".

An example of the inference method will be as follows:

- If you see black smoke, this will be your result.

- And knowing that black smoke is created from fire will be your argument.

- The existence of fire inducing the smoke will be your inferred fact.

'In the first example, the stated fact can also be a result if you want to see what caused the fire and the same can also be done in the second example where the result can be a fact. It all depends on the speaker and how he would like to look at things and where his argument is heading.

'Deduction and inference are the two methods of argumentation. Deduction uses the information provided in the facts to prove an unknown result. Inference uses the information provided in the result to prove the unknown facts. I know this might seem like an unnecessary complication and that the usage of premise statements and conclusion statements might be much easier and direct, but it can be sometimes beneficial.'

'I agree with you that arguments can function on deduction and inference, as you name it,' said Plato. 'And I also see that using the premise-conclusion method is much more direct, but how can the other way be more beneficial?'

'When you use the substitute wordings,' spoke Alfred, 'you are clarifying the purpose of your premises, as either facts or results; and what type of conclusion you are aiming for, which can be of the same categories as the premises. As for the argument, it will be clear which function is being used between deduction and inference.

'This clarification helps in distinguishing the roles of the structure, making it easier for the argumentator to assemble his speech and easier for the listener to follow the point of the speech presented to him.'

'You know what, Alfred,' said Plato, 'I never thought of argumentation in this way. I think I just stuck to the structure of premises and conclusions I was used to.'

'I don't blame you,' said Alfred, 'I think it is because you are almost always surrounded by people who are more intelligent than the average Joe, that you never ran into the problem of someone not following your argument. As for me, I'm quite the opposite: you wouldn't believe the types of people I have to converse with on a daily basis. People that lack, to put it simply, simple logic.'

'You are right in that one, my friend!' replied Plato. 'I'm not sure whether to feel lucky or sorry for myself. But I tend to feel sorry for not having enough experience with other types of people.'

Alfred made a sigh and said, 'You should feel lucky, trust me.'

Alfred and Plato shared a laugh, the kind of laughter that only long-time friends have.

Plato said, 'We just spoke of how argument achieves its function, but we never stated plainly what that function is. Would you care, Alfred, to do that?'

'With pleasure,' said Alfred. 'I see the main function of the argument as to reason and rationalize the premises and how they lead to certain conclusions.'

'I think this sums it up well. What do you think, Luqman?' said Plato.

'I think so as well,' replied Luqman.

'Now, after we have examined all of the premises, arguments, and conclusions, which are the structural parts of the logical speech,' spoke Alfred, 'I think it is about time to divert our attention to Logic and see where it is applicable in this structure.'

'Allow me to carry on the conversation with Alfred, Plato, and answer this question,' requested Luqman.

'Please, by all means,' replied Plato.

'Thank you,' said Luqman. 'Let's start by examining the following two arguments:

The first one is:

- Men are mortals,

- Socrates is a man,

- Therefore, Socrates is mortal.

The second one is:

- Humans drink water,

- Pixie, the cat, drinks water

- Therefore, Pixie is a human.

'Both arguments follow the same structure of having the premise statements at the beginning followed by a conclusion statement based on the premises. Any argument which follows this structure, where the premises and the conclusion are related to each other in the right way, is said to be a valid argument but not necessarily a sound one, because it doesn't regard whether the statements provided are true or false. For an argument to be sound, both of its premises and conclusion have to be true.

'In the first argument, the structure, or relation, is correct and the premises along with the conclusion are true, therefore, the argument is both a valid and a sound one. In the second argument, the structure is correct but not all of the premises and conclusion are true; therefore, the argument is a valid one but not a sound one. Every sound argument is a valid argument but not every valid argument is a sound one. In summary, premises and conclusions contribute to the validity and soundness of arguments.'

'Coming to Logic, the purpose of Logic is to ensure that the argument leads to the correct conclusion. It does so by ensuring that all parts of speech are consistent with truth and facts firstly, and with each other secondly.

'When it comes to the speech parts that Logic is involved in, I see it associated only with arguments and conclusions. When it comes to premises, they cannot be judged on whether they are logical or illogical but only on whether they are true or false for premises consist of facts, and facts can only be judged on the scale of truth and falseness.

'As for the argument and conclusion parts, an argument is how a speaker weaves and relates the premises together to prove a conclusion statement. Taking what we said earlier about the validity and soundness of arguments and concluding statements, in which we see if they make sense or not, we can safely relate arguments and conclusions with logic. Therefore, they can be judged whether they are logical or not.

'Very good, Luqman,' said Plato. 'I agree with what you said about the validity and soundness of an argument. But let me speak about logic in a way more related to conversation and discussion to help us paint a clearer picture.'

To be honest, I found this topic a little bit hard to follow and I was forcing my mind to cope with the conversation. And when Plato said his last sentence, I was happy to hear it, for I really needed something I could relate to, and that is conversations.

'Please, Plato, go ahead,' said Alfred. 'You will be doing us a big favor.'

'A decisive factor in winning a debate or proving a point in a discussion, is the argument used.' Plato continued, 'It is necessary to use a suitable argument related to the topic at hand for the argument to appear logical. Let's see the following example:

- Alligators are reptiles,

- Dragons are reptiles that shoot fire,

- Therefore, alligators shoot fire as well.

In this example, the argument of dragons isn't suitable to be used with alligators since both of them are of different species and their biology doesn't relate.

'An argumentator must always use suitable, related, and logical arguments and must divert away from using irrational, inconsequential, and unreasonable arguments in his speeches.'

Plato's addition really helped in bridging the meaning of the topic to me. At first, I was struggling with the meaning and purpose of Logic, but now it was clear.

'There is another feature of logical argumentation that I think we should examine,' said Alfred.

'What is it?' asked Luqman.

'When making an argument,' spoke Alfred, 'there are two ways that premises can be aligned, so to speak. To make it clearer, let's explore these two ways through the following examples:

The first example is:

- – Men are mortal,

- – Socrates is a man,

- – Therefore, Socrates is mortal.

The second example is:

- – Men are mortal,

- – Socrates is mortal,

- – Therefore, Socrates is a man.

'What do you think about the first example?'

'I see it as a valid, sound, and a logical argument,' replied Luqman.

'What about the second example?' asked Alfred.

'The premises and the conclusion are true, but I find the argument is illogical,' answered Luqman.

'Why is that? Doesn't the argument lead to a truthful and a logical conclusion?' said Alfred.

'It is a truthful one,' replied Luqman, 'but the argument that led to the conclusion is not a logical one; therefore, the conclusion can't be logical. Illogic can never lead to logic.'

'That is true, but do you know why the argument is not logical?' said Alfred.

'Why?' replied Luqman.

'It is all about how the subjects in the premises were presented,' Alfred continued. 'First, let us list the subjects. We have men, Socrates, and mortals, which we will refer to as A, B, and C respectively, for smoother understanding. In the first example, the subjects were presented as follows: A = C, B = A, therefore B = C. While in the second example, the subjects were presented as follows: A = C, B = C, therefore B = A.

A = Men   B = Socrates   C = Mortals

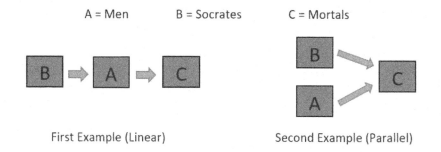

First Example (Linear)   Second Example (Parallel)

'In the first example, the argument was put in a linear fashion while in the other example, the argument was put in a parallel fashion. In the linear fashion, the argumentation works because there was a relation built into the premises between B and C. But in the parallel fashion, there is no relation built between the premises A and B; therefore, stating the conclusion that A = B is illogical even though its premises are true.'

'Could you elaborate more on the linear and parallel fashions; I didn't quite get them,' I requested.

'Of course.' Alfred then reached for a napkin on the table and took out his pen. He started drawing on the piece of napkin and saying, 'In the first example, the first premise, "men are mortal", indicates that men are part of mortality which is shown in the diagram here as the circle of men (A) inside or part of the bigger circle of mortality (C). As for the second premise, "Socrates is a man", it indicates that Socrates is part of men shown in the diagram as the circle of Socrates (B) inside that of men (A). Coming to the conclusion statement, since the circle of Socrates is part of the circle of men, and since the circle of men is part of the circle of mortality, a valid relation was built between the subjects allowing us to say that Socrates is a part of mortality.

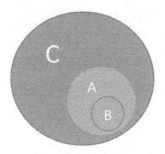 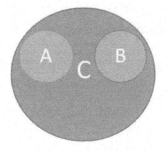

First Example (Linear)   Second Example (Parallel)

'Is the first example clear, Nate?'

'Much clearer. Now, I understand much better,' I replied.

'That is good. Let's move on then to the next example.' Alfred continued, 'In the second example, the first premise, "Men are mortal", indicates
that men are part of mortality which is shown in the diagram here as the
circle of Men (A) inside or part of the circle of mortality (C). In the second
premise, "Socrates is mortal", it indicates that Socrates is a part of mortality
shown in the diagram as the circle B, inside the circle C. As for the conclusion statement, "Therefore, Socrates is a man", it is illogical to come to such
a statement since there was not enough relation built between Socrates and
men. It is true that both of them belong to the same circle of mortality, but
that is not enough to say that either of them equals the other.

'This would be a good example for an argument not being valid due
to the relation between its statements; although they are true, they aren't
presented in a way that leads to the conclusion statement. I called it a parallel
argument because the premises statements, A and B, are equal to each other
and one isn't part of the other.'

'Now, thanks to the diagram you drew,' I spoke, 'things are much clearer
and easier to follow, thank you,'

'My pleasure,' Alfred replied with a smile.

'Nicely said, Alfred,' said Luqman. 'This is a clear explanation of the validity of an argument.'

'The parallel argumentation might work in mathematical formulas. For example, if the lengths of two lines equal a third, then they are equal in length,' said Alfred. 'But in logic, this formula simply doesn't work. A valid relation must be built between the subjects.'

'This is both true and weird,' spoke Plato. 'I've always thought that mathematics was the way to learn and practice Logic.'

'I thought the same thing, too,' said Luqman.

'So far we saw Logic being associated with argumentations and its purpose is to lead to the correct conclusion.' Plato continued, 'I don't have a precise definition to what Logic is yet, but given this finding that Alfred just shed light on, we must look into the relationship between Logic and Mathematics first, before we give a definition to Logic.'

'That is for certain,' said Luqman.

'For me, I don't have that kind of knowledge yet and I need to research the matter before I put forth any opinion or fact,' said Plato. 'But if either of you have something to share, I'm all ears.'

'I, too, need to research this kind of relationship,' said Luqman.

'As for me, my mathematical knowledge is weak; I can't be much of a help in this matter,' said Alfred.

'So, it is decided then,' spoke Plato, 'we leave this topic right now and come back to it later when we have the knowledge it requires.'

'Certainly, we shouldn't leave such an important topic in oblivion,' said Luqman.

'It is as you said,' spoke Alfred, 'and I hope that I can join you when it's time comes.'

'You are always welcome to join us, Alfred,' said Plato.

I found that night's topic, Logic, very interesting and an essential one to understand and use as a philosopher, even though it was hard to understand in some parts. I learned that a crucial element of any argument is for it to be valid, sound, and logical. Until that night, I'd thought a philosopher's speech was measured by the knowledge, wisdom, and truths within it. I had never given logic and argumentation any weight. I considered my learning on this topic to be a great step towards my goal.

One last thing that took my attention was that Plato and the others weren't ashamed or afraid of acknowledging their ignorance of a subject and admitting the need to do more research before giving their answer. It was an honorable gesture, one I was happy to know was an option—even for professionals like Plato.

CHAPTER 11

Research

A few days later, I came to the café hoping to see as many members of the group as possible, but to my disappointment, no one was there and I ended up sitting alone in the café with my coffee cup next to me.

Alfred noticed that I'd been sitting alone for a while and so he came to me and asked, 'What's wrong, my child?'

'It's nothing,' I replied, unfeelingly.

Alfred took a seat at my table and said, 'You look pale. I know there is something. Tell me.'

I stayed silent for a while and then started speaking, 'It's my last day in Paris. Tomorrow, I'm going to fly home and I was hoping to see the group before I leave.'

'That's very sad to hear,' said Alfred, 'especially since I'm getting used to you as part of the group.'

Alfred's words made me smile and I replied, 'Thank you, Alfred. I'm glad to hear that.'

'Where are you from?' asked Alfred.

'I'm from the United States of America,' I answered.

'You're far away from home! What are you doing here?' said Alfred.

'I'm attending my school here, but now it's summer vacation and my family is going back to the States,' I said.

'That's good! It means that you will be back after your vacation is over, right?' said Alfred.

'Yeah,' I replied.

'Then why the pale face?' asked Alfred.

'I just wanted to sit with Plato or any one of his friends and have one last conversation before I leave,' I said.

'Well, this might just be your lucky day,' said Alfred.

'What do you mean?' I asked, confused.

'Look who just came in,' replied Alfred.

I looked in the direction of the café entrance to see that Plato had just entered. I felt a surge of happiness inside of me and I couldn't help but smile.

Plato approached us and said, 'Good afternoon, gentlemen.'

'Good afternoon, Plato,' replied Alfred, standing up. 'Please, Plato, have my seat and I'll bring your usual order.'

'Why don't you join us, Alfred?' offered Plato.

'You're too kind, sir,' replied Alfred. 'I would, but I have work to get back to.'

'Thank you, Alfred,' replied Plato, taking Alfred's seat.

'How are you today, Nate?' said Plato.

'I'm… I'm fine,' I replied, trying to suppress my sadness as hard as I could.

'What's wrong?' asked Plato with a serious look on his face.

I hesitated at first, but then I felt that he would insist even more and so I told him the whole story.

'I understand now,' said Plato. 'In that case, I think I have a topic that will be most useful to you during your summer vacation.'

'What is it?' I asked curiously.

'It is about how to do research and how to acquire knowledge correctly,' answered Plato.

'That would be really awesome!' I said enthusiastically. 'This way, I could fill my free time during the vacation learning about different stuff and when I come back later, I'll be a better speaker and maybe I'll teach one thing or two.'

Plato smiled and said, 'Sure, sure! I look forward to it.'

'So, please, teach me,' I said.

'My pleasure,' said Plato. 'Just to let you know from the start, this won't be the usual long topic we usually discuss where every point leads to the next. Instead, it will be a handful of points that won't necessarily connect with each other directly. But they will serve the overall topic, which is how to research in a way that you'll be sure you have obtained the correct knowledge.'

'That's totally fine,' I replied.

'Let's start with the first point,' Plato said, 'if you hear an opinion or an explanation regarding a topic that is new to you and you have no previous knowledge of it, how do you know if that opinion is right or wrong?'

Oh my god, Plato doesn't take his time, I thought. He immediately fires with all cylinders. I didn't expect this kind of question from the get-go.

'Well, I would have to listen to the logic of the opinion before I make that kind of judgement,' I replied, after taking a few moments to think Plato's question over.

'Why is that?' asked Plato.

'Because if the opinion lacks logic, then it must be wrong,' I answered. 'But if the opinion is logical, then it is right.'

'So far, so good,' said Plato. 'Tell me, Nate, don't we find in some of the scientific fields of today some topics that have gone through many theories throughout the centuries until reaching their modern concept? For example, the shape of the Earth, the shape of the universe, cell theory, diseases and remedies, and so on?'

'Yes, we do, and there are plenty of them,' I replied.

'Taking the theory of the Earth and the solar system as an example,' Plato continued, 'didn't the universe go through multiple theories regarding its shape, starting with the Jewish concept of an Earth wide as the whole universe with the heavenly dome above it and Shoel, or the underworld, below it. After this, came the theory of the geocentric model of the universe where the Earth is a round body surrounded by an orbiting sun, moon, and the seven planets of antiquity. Then, came the heliocentric model we know today of the sun at the center being orbited by the planets.

'Don't all of those three models I just mentioned have a rich body of knowledge and explanations suitable to them at the time of their conception and birth?'

'Yes, they do,' I replied.

Plato continued, 'Don't those models include a lot of systematic details which explain how their universe is run? And don't those systems have interconnected reasons and explanations of why they are the way they are?'

'Yes, they do,' I replied.

Plato continued, 'Considering the period of time in history in which each of those theories or models were introduced, along with the knowledge that was common among the people, would you say that the theories seemed logical to the people of that time?'

'Well, if I was living at the time when each theory was introduced, I think I'd find each one of them logical,' I said.

'And if they are logical, then they must be true, right?' asked Plato.

'Yes, they should be,' I answered.

'So now, all of the three theories are both true and logical?' said Plato.

'At the time of their conception, yes,' I replied.

Plato continued, 'But in reality, only one is true, or right, while the other two are wrong, correct?'

'That is correct,' I replied.

Plato continued, 'So, we have a theory or an opinion that is both logical and wrong, right?'

'It isn't logical,' I said. 'It only seemed that way because the correct, or the more logical, model wasn't known at that time. That's why the false one seemed logical and right.'

'Very perceptive, Nate!' said Plato. 'Do you know what that means?'

I thought for a moment and said, 'I'm not sure.'

'That's fine,' spoke Plato. 'Tell me now, if you had no previous knowledge of the shape of the universe and you heard the geocentric and heliocentric theories, would you be able to tell which one of the two is the correct one?'

'Yes, I would,' I replied.

'Why?' asked Plato.

I answered, 'Because the right one would seem more logical than the wrong one. At least, it should be that way according to our logic so far.'

'You are absolutely correct,' said Plato. 'Do you know what that means?'

I smiled at Plato and said, 'No!'

'That's fine, let me explain it to you.' Plato continued, 'It is in the nature of the mind that when hearing a well-thought-out explanation or an opinion about something, which the mind has no previous knowledge of, to see it as a logical opinion and, therefore, right and true even if the opinion is wrong. The mind would make that assumption because, with no previous knowledge about the topic, it has nothing to refer or to compare the newly heard opinion to and thus it will find it logical.

'To make this point clearer, let us examine a hypothetical question. Let's assume that, regarding a random topic, which you have no previous knowledge of, there are three theories about it and you've heard of one of them. Can you tell whether this theory is right or not?'

'No,' I replied.

'What about after you hear a second theory,' said Plato. 'Can you tell which one is right and which is wrong?'

'No, not yet,' I said. 'I need to hear all of the three theories so I can recognize and distinguish the right theory from the false ones.'

'You are right,' said Plato. 'In general, in order to know which theory or opinion is right or wrong, you need to hear all of the other opinions and then determine which one is the most logical one. You see, to know the right opinion, you need to hear all of the false ones, otherwise there will be no way of ensuring that the opinion you came across is the right one or not. For even the argument of the wrong opinion might seem logical enough to be the truth, if the argument of the right opinion isn't heard. In conclusion, by hearing and knowing the logic of the false opinions, only then will you be able to recognize the right one.

'Having said that, let me highlight a very important fact here. Righteousness needs falseness to speak out so it gets known, while falseness must suppress righteousness so it doesn't get exposed. Thus, it is very important to hear all of the opinions regarding a subject before making a judgement of which opinion is right and which is wrong. Is this clear?'

'Yes, it is very clear and logical, Plato,' I replied.

'All right then, let's move on to how you should use this information while researching any topic.' Plato continued, 'Aside from hearing all of the opinions regarding a topic, there is a way that could help you determine if the opinion is right or wrong, and that way is what I mentioned earlier about falseness needing to suppress righteousness. This method is particularly useful when hearing a debate or a conversation between people or having them yourself with someone else. By seeing a person trying to suppress the opinion of others—like by interrupting them and not letting them speak— you will be able to assume that he is wrong and most of the time you will be correct in doing that.

'A huge factor in determining whether your opinion is right or wrong is your manners. It doesn't matter if you are right, if you resemble those manners of false opinions—like bad- mouthing or interrupting your oppo- nent—your right opinion will look like a false one. Remember, if you're right, you need your opponent to speak out his version of the truth so yours gets recognized. Even if your opponent interrupts you and disrespects you, never fight back; in fact, you should be thanking him, for he is doing you a big favor by sharing his opinion and behaving like this.

'And thus, our first point ends here. I hope you understood it well.'

I replied, 'I understand what you're saying very well from many per- sonal experiences with people that behaved exactly how you described a man with a false opinion would.'

'Very good. Let's move on to the second point which regards argu- mentation,' spoke Plato. 'Whilst researching for information or knowledge in one topic, we come across all sorts of theories and explanations that either contradict each other or go in their own separate ways. A question must be asked here which is how do we know which theory or explanation is correct and which is wrong.

'The method we spoke about in the previous point helps while listening to or speaking with other people, but what if your research involved written materials, recorded speeches, or video lectures, how can you then know which explanation is right or which theory is wrong? Any speech or work designed to deliver new information should go through the structure of the logic speech, which is facts, argument, and the intended result.

'So, the first thing to watch out for is anyone delivering new information to you and not following the logic speech. In that case, he is forcing the information on to you, instead of rationalizing it. This is a direct indicator that what he's saying is probably false and can't be rationalized, and that is why he is using the authority method of conveying the information.

'The second, and most important thing, is regarding the argumentation of the speech itself. Know this: everyone can make an argument but not every argument is logical, and it is through logic that correct knowledge is known. Right now, we will examine a couple of common argumentations together.'

'Go ahead, Plato, I'm all ears,' I said.

Plato continued with, 'Tell me, in any field of study, if you earn a bachelor degree in it and, later, you follow your degree with a master's and a doctor of philosophy degree, what does that make you?'

'A professional or an expert in that field of study,' I replied. 'Is that what you mean?'

'It is,' said Plato. 'And having obtained all of these degrees, you must have learned and gained a lot of knowledge in your field of study, isn't this right?'

'Supposedly,' I replied.

Plato continued with, 'Let's say that you were conversing with someone and you wanted to convince him about something, and in doing so, you used your expertise as the logic of your argumentation. Now, is this a good argument or not?'

'I think it is,' I replied.

'Even if the argument lacks the explanation or the reasoning part?' asked Plato.

'Even if it lacks those,' I started answering, 'the expertise title carries with it all of the years of experience and knowledge and that will, or should, suffice.'

'You are right in what the title conveys,' said Plato. 'But will it be enough to substitute reason and explanation?

I stayed silent and didn't reply.

'Will arguments based on titles of expertise always lead to the right opinion or knowledge?' asked Plato.

'Not always, for I see some experts with wrong opinions,' I answered.

'Is it a reliable or an unreliable argumentation method then?' asked Plato.

'If it doesn't work all of the time, then it is unreliable,' I answered

'Therefor, expertise titles shouldn't be used as the logic of the argument,' said Plato.

'I agree with you,' I spoke, 'but I see both reason and explanation share the same unreliability as expertise titles in which not every reason and explanation is correct.'

'You are absolutely right,' spoke Plato. 'In reason and explanation, you can judge whether they are right or wrong based on the logic they carry. But when it comes to titles, there is nothing to inspect and hold against logic, thus they are not associated with what is logical and what is illogical.

'That being so, you should never accept an argument based on titles only, nor should you ever give one,' said Plato. 'Instead, judge the argument based on its reason and explanation and then assess it on the scale of logic.'

'You are right,' I said.

'Let's examine one more common argument used,' spoke Plato. 'You mentioned earlier that the number of degrees held relates to the experience one has, correct?'

'That is correct,' I replied.

'What about the number of years spent studying a subject? Would this also relate to the experience gained?' asked Plato.

'Yes, it would and I think I know where you are going with this,' I spoke. 'The argument made with the expertise titles can also be applied to that of the number of years of experience—is that right?'

'Clever boy! That is exactly where I was going with my example,' said Plato. 'So you understand that the number of years of experience isn't related to logic, just like titles, right?'

'Yes, I understand,' I replied.

'To conclude the second point, never accept any piece of knowledge or information without a logical argument,' spoke Plato. 'For it is through logical argumentation that you judge whether knowledge is right or wrong. And remember, no matter how many titles you have on your name, or how many years you've spent practicing and studying a subject, it doesn't matter when it comes to logical argumentation, because titles and years are not valid arguments and have nothing to do with logic. What is important at the end is the logical reasoning and explanation behind your argument. Is the second point clear?'

'It is all clear, Plato,' I replied.

'Very good. Now, let's start with the third point,' said Plato. 'So far we've spoken about the manners of speaking and the speech itself but now it is about time we looked into how to choose the person to ask, or how to obtain the knowledge you are researching and looking for. Now, in such a position, the expertise and the number of years spent practicing or studying any subject will be the thing to look for.'

'But didn't we just agree that years and expertise don't amount to anything?' I asked.

'That's not entirely true,' answered Plato. 'The area where expertise and years are worthless in is argumentation, for they lack logic in the first place. But when it comes to who you should seek for your questions, they are the only factors to consider. To make it clearer, answer me the following questions: when you want to learn about medicine, who should you ask—a doctor or an engineer?'

'The doctor, of course,' I replied.

'And if you want to learn something in carpentry, will you ask a carpenter or a blacksmith?' said Plato.

'I'll ask the carpenter,' I replied.

'Why did you choose your answers the way you did and not the other way around?' asked Plato.

'Because in both questions the other choice had nothing to do with what I wanted to learn,' I answered.

'Right,' spoke Plato, 'you see, in your quest for knowledge, you went to, and preferred, whoever was the expert in the field of study or the skilled practitioner in the craft you wanted to learn something in.'

'That is correct,' I said.

'Let's assume you wanted to know something about farming,' spoke Plato, 'but this time your options are two farmers—one who has been practicing farming for two decades whilst the other farmer has been practicing for only one decade. Now, which of the two farmers would you go to for your question?'

'I think I'd prefer to go to the first farmer,' I replied.

'Why is that?' asked Plato.

'Because he has more experience than the other farmer, and so, he is more likely to answer my question correctly,' I said.

'That is correct.' Plato then said, 'You see, when it comes to experts in any similar field, the next decisive factor will be the number of years of experience one has. It is only reasonable to think that the more time one spends on something, the more experience he'll gain, and thus, the more likely he will have the right knowledge. Although, this is not always true.

'When choosing the right person to ask, the expertise of the individual in the field of study along with the years of experience are two factors that have been proven to be helpful during the selection process. But remember, expertise and experience don't amount to anything when it comes to argumentation, or proving something is right or wrong. What is decisive at that point is the logical reasoning behind the argument. So, someone without expertise and experience is not necessarily false. You need to listen to his argument and then judge accordingly.

'You also need to be selective and cautious with whom you ask, for you can't just ask anyone anything. You need to choose the person to ask carefully and, based on his level of expertise, choose what to ask him. You shouldn't ask someone something not in his or her particular field of knowledge or ask an apprentice something that is within the specialty of the masters. Who you ask is as important as the answer itself and it can even be considered as half of it.

'With this, the third and final point comes to an end. I hope you understood it well and will benefit from our conversation on how to research for knowledge.'

'The last point is very clear,' I said, 'and regarding the conversation, I find all of the points you mentioned true and logical; this is what should be done.'

'Very good.' Then Plato continued talking with a somewhat sad tone, 'Well... I guess this concludes our last conversation.'

'Not to worry,' I spoke. 'I'll be coming back after my summer vacation.'

'That is good to hear,' replied Plato, perking up. 'I forgot that you mentioned it.'

'I'm also happy about that!' I said.

Plato leaned back on his chair and said, 'So, what do you think of the group so far?'

I smiled while I collected my thoughts and said, 'I honestly don't know if I'll be able to say what I am feeling, but I'll try my best. Before I met you, I was walking in life without a purpose like a lost soul, without passion. I yearned to belong somewhere and I'd tried many things, but nothing caught my attention or entered my heart—until I met you and the rest of the group.

'I never thought the topics of Knowledge, Wisdom, Logic, and Philosophy would be so captivating. I don't know why and how, but I found myself drawn to these kinds of topics and conversations even though I thought I never would be. I've always taken speech for granted and never imagined its wide potential and importance. It is as you said in our first meeting: the value of a person is his mind. And the mind is translated through actions and manners and through speech and writing. The mind is truly the most valuable thing in humans.

'Sitting with you and the group and listening to your conversations and arguments have changed me a lot and opened my mind to a new part of life. Thank you very much for that.'

Plato smiled gently and said, 'My son, with all of the distractions and entertainment in the world we live in, it is hard to find someone who is passionate about the art of speech. Most people don't give it any attention and consider it worthless. And, in our time, I see dumbness and stupidity have a higher reputation and value than logical speech.

'A dream of any philosopher is to be able to guide a lost soul into the love of philosophy. I can't describe to you how proud I am of you and happy that you chose to follow the path of philosophy. And I can say for certain that you have become a philosopher.'

'You're being too kind. I'm still too young and inexperienced to become a philosopher like you,' I said.

'Do you know what philosophy is and what it means to be a philosopher?' asked Plato.

I was about to answer, but then I noticed that, of all the topics discussed, the meaning of philosophy had never been addressed directly in any discussion. At that moment, I came to the realization that I didn't exactly know the purpose I had set for my life and there was the possibility that I might have gone astray from what I really wanted. So, I redirected Plato's question to him, eager to hear his answer.

Plato started answering saying, 'Basically, a philosopher is a seeker or pursuer of wisdom, thus making the meaning of philosophy as the pursuit of wisdom. But, since one only seeks after the things he loves, it is more fitting to say that philosophy is the love of wisdom, and a philosopher a lover of wisdom. The word philosophy consists of two Greek words: *philo* meaning loving, and *Sophia* meaning Wisdom. Hence the name *philosophia* that means love of wisdom, which later came to the English language as "philosophy". And so earlier, I wasn't exaggerating when I said that you are a philosopher. You are one by meaning but still not by title.'

'What do you mean?' I said.

'You are a lover and a seeker of wisdom; therefore, you are a philosopher,' said Plato. 'Also know this: the journey of the philosopher is long and never-ending. It's a lifetime quest. So, you need to be patient and determined in seeking after it.'

Plato's words comforted me and relieved me from my earlier concerns. Also, his acknowledgement of me as a philosopher, even by his meaning, meant the world to me. It was a proof and a credit, indicating that I had achieved what I was looking for in the first place; I was on the correct path.

It was as Plato said, philosophy is a life journey and I wasn't planning on stopping anytime soon. I would go home and I wouldn't waste my time playing around. I would learn and learn and I'd come back next year, ready to take Plato and the others head-on in conversations. It was such a relief to have found my purpose and true calling. Now, I could push forward in my life towards something I believed in.

About the Author

M. A. Alsadah has a love for world-building, story-writing and Philosophy. He has published a high-fantasy novel titled "The Seal: the five Metals" in which he invented 2 languages for. He also developed and published a story-focus game on steam titled "Sky Realm: Essences".

Also by
M. A. Alsadah

NOVELS

The Seal: The Five Metals

VIDEO GAMES

Sky Realms: Essences